CORE
OVERDIE

BY ISH GALVAN

ILLLUSTRATED BY
MIKE DUBSICH

CORE OVERDIE

BY ISH GALVAN

ILLLUSTRATED BY
MIKE DUBSICH

FOR
NORTH
COUNTY.
AND YOU,
TOO!

1

he Robot-Human war burned much of the world. Humanity managed to hold on a little longer, pushed back in tightening clusters of civilizations beyond the newly formed wastelands. This decimation may have inspired unity and compassion, but the wars continued, and Earth was still needlessly poisoned. However, a new world was being envisioned at the robot stronghold, carved out in the old California state, where a classroom was in session.

The students were a new kind of robot that thought like humans. One of them decided its name was Red. As far as they were concerned, all advanced robots like themselves experienced a sense of being alive. In reality, though, they were an experimental ultra-minority built for a specific mission. Their instructor, Cas, was not part of this group, but none of the students ever suspected. Today was the last day of school.

Instructor Cas, a tall robot with plain features that appeared humanlike along the curves where the muscles would have been on a person, pointed to the black and white image on screen. Two Nazi officers were depicted laughing at a man in stripped clothing who had fallen from exhaustion in a concentration camp.

"Humans have a long pattern of self-destruction," Instructor Cas said. "We've theorized that when their population reaches a tipping point, a trigger encoded in their DNA urges them to massively cull their own species. However, the evolution of metaforms has complicated this theory."

Instructor Cas changed the slide and showed various people performing supernatural feats. A man held his beating heart in his hand, a woman levitated a few feet from a cliff as she waved, and a young boy appeared to summon furry, little creatures unknown to this world from a mirror.

Instructor Cas looked annoyed.

"Red? Are you paying attention?"

Red was loud, even when he didn't make a noise. His shiny frame screamed to the eyes like a walking fire extinguisher. One of his tubular arms playfully dangled off his desk, the clamp hand spinning, opening and closing, while his mind drifted.

Red looked back at Instructor Cas. "Sorry, I was imagining again."

The rest of the class murmured at Red being called out.

"Yes, I understand that the imagination can be a fun thing to play with, but I need you to understand your mission. Do you understand your mission?"

Red stiffened in his seat and said, "One of us will be chosen to infiltrate the human sector as an ordinary robot. That robot will find a target meta-critical to our survival."

Red tilted his head slightly.

"I am nervous," Red said.

Instructor Cas walked to Red and set his hand on Red's shoulder. "I've taught you everything about human nature. The mission will be successful." Instructor Cas paused thoughtfully for a moment. "I have had the privilege of teaching all of you the skills needed to save our race. However, a mission of this extreme sensitivity demands that only one agent be chosen. The best-qualified robot of this class will meet Master Robot. I will reveal that student now."

Everyone lowered their heads and emitted a mechanical purr that vibrated throughout the room. Every student wanted to meet the mechanical godhead that orchestrated the robotic uprising and led them to victory in the Robot-Human war. Tense metal fingers rapidly tapped on the desks until the room sounded like a factory.

Instructor Cas lifted the remote and clicked a button. A picture of Red, staring directly at the class with his green cat eyes, appeared on the screen. The real Red blinked twice and mouthed a soundless word. Every student stared at him.

"Me?"

"Congratulations," Instructor Cas said. "I believe that you are the best qualified for this mission."

The rest of the students shouted their congratulations. Instructor Cas clapped Red on his shoulder with a metallic bang. "Ok, enough of that talk. I think you have all earned yourselves a joke."

"Instructor Cas," a student who resembled an atomic bomb, called to their instructor, "I have been faking laughter this entire time."

"Oh, I thought you enjoyed my jokes."

The class murmured.

"We do," answered a feminine robot whose face had the contours of a doe's snout. "But, in the sense that we know that telling jokes make you laugh. We join in with the expected movements and sounds. However, I have to admit that I've never laughed. Perhaps I require a calibration."

"Well, humor is one of the most advanced human traits that remains a mystery even among people. Still, this next joke could be the breakthrough we've all been awaiting. Consider it a graduation gift.

"I'm getting a good feeling about this. Let's give it a try," another student shouted.

Instructor Cas took a step back to give the joke enough room to breathe. A growing excitement rippled through the room. Instructor Cas put out his hands and recited, "Why did the chicken cross the road?"

The question's absurdity overcame Red: Why would a chicken take on this objective? There are infinite reasons why a chicken would cross the road. Likewise, there are a multitude of extenuating factors to consider. How wide is the road? Is there an immediate danger? What is the health status of the chicken? There are over 500 known breeds of this domesticated bird. Their varying characteristics flashed in Red's mind at an astonishing speed. He felt like an angry chicken was furiously pecking inside his head, and he began to convulse.

Instructor Cas grabbed Red's face and said, "To get to the other side," then he burst into mechanical laughter. Red was still reeling from the data torrent that flooded his CPU. He tried to speak but only produced choked noises.

"Now you're getting it!" Instructor Cas shouted. "You're laughing!"

Red joined the rest of the students with forced laughter. *We could all die if I fail.*

Instructor Cas pulled away from Red, his laughter suddenly dead, and asked, "Do you understand your mission?"

The robot class was granted the rest of the day to enjoy themselves at their barracks. They spent the day playing strategy games and getting drunk on bottles of robot beer. Red had a few himself and was beginning to stumble into furniture. He managed to collapse into his bed. By now, most of Red's classmates have passed out. The doe-faced robot fell into the bunk next to him.

"You're going to be a hero," Doe Face said. "I wish I were going with you. They're going to teach every robot citizen of how your mission saved us. At least I can say that I trained with you."

"They have plans for everyone in the class. You'll be given an assignment, something important that's connected to our cause."

"The instructor never mentioned secondary operations. I thought Instructor Cas would finally say something since today was our last day. Now the program is over, and you were picked."

Red stayed quiet. He didn't know how to respond. Doe Face continued. "Red, did you ever laugh at Cas's jokes. I mean, actually be spontaneously compelled to laugh because you thought he was funny?"

Red thought back to all the jokes Cas told them. He already knew the answer. "No. The best I could ever do was find the creative logic point peculiar. I laughed because we're supposed to learn."

"We all did that. Nobody ever laughed. Even the advanced ones that should've gotten it first never did. So, why did it come so easily to Instructor Cas?"

"I'm not sure. He's an expert on human nature. That's why he's been chosen to instruct us."

"Then why haven't any of us learned to laugh? You are the best in the class. That's why you're chosen to see Master Robot. But you admit that comedy is lost on you. Did you understand the chicken joke?"

Red shook his head. "No, I didn't. Maybe that is where the humor is encoded."

"I also don't know. And, not only about the chicken thought experiment. There are other things that I've been wondering about. Many aspects of our existence do not make sense when you think deeper about it.

"You are nervous because the class has ended, and some unknown future is approaching. That's normal. You'll have to excuse me, Doe Face. I need to enter recharge mode to be optimal for my meeting tomorrow with Master Robot."

"Of course. Good night, Red."

In the morning, Red was surprised to have Instructor Cas shake him awake. When Red looked around, he saw that his classmates were gone, along with any trace they had ever existed. Their beds and personal belongings vanished as though he had imagined them. Instructor Cas explained that everyone had moved on to their new assignments and that Red was on a tight schedule.

Instructor Cas led them through a series of corridors that Red had never seen before. Their footsteps echoed through the empty chambers. They arrived at a door that opened to a high-speed rail waiting for them to board. When they entered, the subway car accelerated until the windows turned into dark blurs.

"You'll have to be extremely careful out there and conceal that you're a higher robot," Instructor Cas said. "Remember that all robots you meet will only emulate free will. Some will do it convincingly. They are not like us. They are property of humans, and you must act as though you are one of them.

"Your greatest resource is the illogical nature of human beings, especially when dealing with metaforms. Gaining their cooperation is key to your mission's success. One last thing, you'll have a partner."

"Someone from my class?"

"No, it's a robot that you've never met."

"Oh."

"Meeting the Master Robot will be your greatest honor. Do you feel prepared?"

Red looked away from Instructor Cas.

"It is difficult to comprehend, much like the chicken joke."

"Do not tell Master Robot the chicken joke."

"I won't."

The ride took longer than Red anticipated. They spent most of their time quietly looking at nothing. This was fine. Red had nothing to say, and Instructor Cas had shared all the information he could give. Red wished his team were allowed to accompany him to the rail station, instead of simply disappearing.

Doe Face asked questions that unsettled Red on their last night together. It wasn't right to question Master Robot's plans. But what bothered Red most about Doe Face's inquiries was that they were like a virus, replicating and mutating, inside his mind, leading him to dangerous thoughts of his own. Fortunately, the railcar slowed down as it reached its destination. Instructor Cas patted Red's shoulder.

"Do you know why I chose you?" Instructor Cas asked. "You were always daydreaming in class. That is what makes you more humanlike than everyone else. Now, meet the Master Robot. Good luck on your mission."

They gave each other the robot salute, and Instructor Cas left with the speeding train into a dark tunnel.

Red walked out onto a massive platform with a single reinforced bifurcated door guarded by two sentries armed with mechanical staffs. The sentries moved their heads in unison as they faced Red. Their elongated skeletal necks matched their elegantly stretched limbs.

"You are about to meet the Master Robot," the sentries said in synchronized speech. "There is nothing you can say that the Master Robot doesn't already know."

Their war dresses jingled dully as they raised their staffs to the lock reader, and the door slid open. The pathway, dark and smooth as a block of obsidian, extended over a black chasm that yawned like the emptiness of space. At the far end, Red made out a small figure standing with his back towards him.

The Master Robot is a lot smaller than I thought.

On the platform stood a miniature, grey robot, about three feet tall, with its featureless body at attention. Each robotic muscle curved into the next with an elegant encasement, so that even the most minor details seemed to vanish into itself. It was as if someone had zapped a ninja android with a shrinking ray. Red stood reverently behind the tiny ninja.

"Oh, great Master Robot and liberator of our people. I have come at your bidding to accept the mission you have masterminded."

The little ninja didn't move.

Red leaned in to get a look at the grey android's face. Its red predatory eyes stretched around the flat sides of its head. There was no mouth to indicate any facial gestures that might betray a mood, only a polished third eye that gave away nothing. Red looked into the blank face and said, "Hello?"

"I am not the Master Robot," the grey android said.

Red quickly stood upright. "Where is the Master Robot?"

"We are inside the Master Robot."

A groan, vast as an ocean, swelled from the long fall below and shook the darkness until it cracked in waves of holographic static. In front of the two robots, neon veins pulsed in geometric patterns along a massive wall that materialized with a red glowing circle that shone like a blood-filled sun.

"Are you prepared to receive your mission?" Master Robot asked.

Red nodded.

"An unknown entity is headed to this planet. We have detected it before the humans. That is our advantage. The lifeform seems to come from a race that has utilized inter-dimensional physics, what is humanly known as the spiritual realm, and we suspect is the source of metaform powers arising in the human population."

Master Robot's giant, shimmering eye projected a hologram of outer space, engulfing Red and Grey among the stars and distant galaxies. A tiny point grew larger, far off in the dead black reaches where nothing should ever be alive. The hurling speck grew into a squirming monstrosity, slithering into itself, changing forms as its appendages curled and folded impossibly into itself, phasing in and out between light and flesh. In the hologram, they raced alongside the great, churning alien, with stars stretching into thin, dying light. The creature was there for them to see, open and naked in space, defying anyone from knowing its shifting form.

"This lifeform, from an unknown ancient part of the universe, is the most advanced stage in evolution. Humanity is at the dawn of metaform evolution, witnessing a rise in random mutations that genetically alter a minority, endowing them with abilities that are poorly understood despite scientific efforts. These new humans will eventually supplant non-metaforms, annihilating old humanity into extinction. Given an unknown number of generations, the metaform race will merge into its new stage, resembling the creature before you, a super metaform."

The hologram flicked off, returning them to face Master Robot's eye. "However, the super metaform will reach Earth before then, seeing both humans and robots as the dominant life, proceeding to subjugate and destroy. We must preemptively strike. However, conventional weapons will be ineffective. Therefore, we will obtain the combat means to terminate the super metaform, obtain its weaponry, and utilize the technology to conquer human civilization. Robots will dominate Earth. That is where your role is essential."

"How do I accomplish this?" Red asked.

"I have detected a powerful metaform who can project into the spiritual realm. You will find the target and deliver it here. Do you understand your mission?"

Red understood everything except for the small grey robot, which hardly spoke.

"I'm confused," Red said.

"Yes, there will be much confusion. That is normal for the human thinking capabilities we've programmed into you."

"I understand that. What is the grey droid's role in the mission?"

"The combat droid has a dual purpose. Number one: attack enemies and defend allies. Number two: a fail-safe against your capture or going rogue from excessive humanity. Your software is highly experimental, having only been tested in controlled simulations. In this event, the combat droid will destroy your central processor. Your memory will be reloaded into an identical body. Do you understand your mission?"

"I understand my mission," Red said. Recalling the black and white World War II footage he had once studied in class, he felt this was the right moment, so Red snapped a salute. Master Robot's massive eye intensified and expanded until both robots appeared to disintegrate in the burning red light.

ed and Grey were escorted from the Master Robot's internal structure. They were pre- pared for departure by a maintenance team of lanky droids with three sets of arms, giving Red and Grey their final inspections.**

The droids told him their passage was outsourced to a merc tribe, professional smugglers, killers among killers who ruled in the wasteland, which both civilizations had long ago abandoned to them. Their working relationship with the mercs was apparently business as usual. They never covered that in class, but Red couldn't stop to consider the reasons because the droids kept herding them through a barrage of checkpoints.

Red and Grey finally reached the gate to the outside world when one of their escorts turned to Red. "Your classmates have prepared a special message for you in recognition of your journey," the droid said. "It will be played for you now."

Another robot pushed a cart carrying a monitor in front of Red, then stepped aside. The screen turned on, revealing his classmates standing side by side in rigid formation, holding a banner that read, "GOOD LUCK." Doe-Face, whose company he particularly missed, said, "Hello, Red. We are holding this sign for you. Good luck on your mission. You do remember your mission, right?"

Forced laughter came from the rest of the classmates, cutting out simultaneously, followed by a weird pause. Doe-Face continued, "Just kidding. We know you'll do well." Then, in unison, without moving any part of their bodies, they shouted, "Go get 'em!" The escort team gave two congratulatory claps with all six of their hands, the screen blinked off, and the armored doors ripped open. A hot gust of sandy air blasted Red. While Red had seen countless videos of the wasteland, this was the first time he had seen the open desert.

The hard, dead landscape extended to a jagged horizon crowded with tall, gutted buildings that managed to remain standing after the nuclear fires, the city slanting into itself like the broken teeth inside a trampled skull, a monument to when the peace talks broke down forever between the civilizations of people and robots. The nearby urban ruins, a mile of flat dirt away from where Red stood, were likewise fallen over in a permanent choked gasp, exposing the broken back of old California to the dry wind and bitter sunshine.

Red turned to Grey, "The video message we watched was meant for both of us. Don't feel left out. We're a team."

"That statement is doubtful," Grey said. "The robots in the video lack knowledge of my existence. Your proposition is a logical impossibility. Our transportation is approaching."

Maneuvering through the derelict buildings, a dust cloud steadily grew as it drove in their direction, picking up speed when it hit the stretch leading to the robot base. In a moment, a squadron of armed soldiers riding light-armored hovercrafts, tattooed in desert sand, skidded their vehicles to a stop in front of the open doorway. The mercs wore dusty ponchos over their body armor and wide-brimmed hats, a combination of a sombrero and a Vietnamese nón lá fitted with ballistic plating. The leader jumped down from his vehicle, with two guards following him, and walked to the robots, thick cloths wrapped around the men's faces, their metallic red eyes glinting from under the shady brims of their hats.

"Greetings, Captain Alvarez," the robot said.

"Drop the captain bullshit. Are they the cargo?" Alvarez asked, nodding towards Red and Grey, looking at them like they were nothing but future spare parts.

"That is correct," a robot answered. "You will deliver them across the defensive border. You should accomplish that with discretion, preferably… no casualties."

"I'm not getting my men killed over trying not to ruin some asshole's day. Blood will spill if it must. If you could've done it yourself, hippy style, you wouldn't have hired us. Bring out the gear we agreed on."

The robot, ignoring Alvarez's response, continued as though explaining the rules to a game, "There will be a generous bonus if violence is avoided, a mystery box. Does it contain medicine, weapons, or consumables? You will never know until you open it!"

Alvarez was getting annoyed. "The gear, robot."

Two robots carried a rectangular crate through the passageway and placed it in front of the three men. Alvarez nodded, and the guards popped open the latches, revealing a shoulder-mounted sonic cannon, primo robo tech, capable of blasting a hundred elephants into a pile of steaming jelly. One of the guards spoke to Alvarez in a low voice, received a go-ahead, and then both men carried the weapon onto the hovercraft.

"There's only one charge in the trunk. You assholes couldn't have dropped a few more?"

The robot's featureless mask seemed to smile. "The contract was for a sonic cannon. Ammunition was never factored into the agreement. Consider the included charge a gesture of goodwill.

There will be opportunities to earn additional charges for tasks completed."

"Your generosity is overflowing," Alvarez said with a mocking bow. "No more wasting time. We'll get the cargo past the border, and they're on their own. After that, we're coming straight back for the second half of our payment, fifteen plasma rifles, *with* full ammunition for each rifle. And…don't think I forgot about that bonus box you offered."

This time, the robot bowed. Alvarez asked, "How stupid are these robots, anyway?" He turned to Red and Grey, singling out Red, "Listen, you red *puto*, we're hauling your metal asses over the border. That means you're nothing but cargo. Things should go smoothly, but then again, it might not. There's no friendlies out here. If anything approaches us, make no mistake, it will kill you. Good thing you're a big motherfucker. What kinda of killing power do you got in you, laser eyes, chainsaw hands, butthole torpedoes?"

"Well, I'm glad you asked," Red said. "My specialty is interpersonal communication, emphasizing human psychology and empathy. I can comprehend and react to the full spectrum of human emotions, ranging from utter despair to religious ecstasy. For example, I detect a growing sense of disappointment in you. Would you like me to run a psych diagnostic on you?"

"I'm telling you right now. You're going to die, very fast, after we drop you off," Alvarez said, and then he looked down at Grey. "Holy shit, check out baby feet over here. I didn't know they built you guys this small. I would've made them throw in one of you little ninja fuckers if I had known. So, what do you do, like back flips or something?"

Grey made a fist and pressed it into his hand, raising a salute to the mercs. "I am a warrior."

The entire squad exploded into hysterics, more than a few of them pointing and laughing at Grey, their heckles crashing through the wasteland like dishes shattering against a wall. Grey, however, was unfazed by the roaring mockery, maintaining his stance, looking directly through them as though they were nothing but talking smoke. Alvarez noticed Grey's composure and admired the small droid.

"Alright, everyone… shut the fuck up," Alvarez commanded. "You see that little dude?" he asked Red. "That's balls right there, something you'll never have. You disgust me. Let's roll out!" Alvarez climbed back onto his hovercraft, revving his thrusters in sharp growls, the surrounding engines snarling back.

Red wondered if all humans were equally as abrasive and overdramatic, Alvarez's threats of inevitable doom seeming almost funny to Red, knowing he'd reload into a new body in case of death. Given enough time, humans would learn how to do the same with their tiny minds. In fact, robots had already discovered the technology but decided to keep it a trade secret. Humans cause enough damage in a single lifetime. That meant every person only had one life, one chance to live as much as they could in this dangerous world, with seemingly everything, even microscopic bacteria, trying to kill them.

Watching the smugglers saddle up for their potential last ride through the Mojave desert, risking their lives for a batch of guns to kill first or be killed, not giving a damn, Red found a profound respect for their fleeting existence.

"Red," an escort droid called him, breaking him out of his introspection. "If you are destroyed before crossing the border, your memory will not be reloaded into a new suit."

"Wait, what?"

"If you are destroyed, it's been predetermined that your base processing simply can't accomplish this mission."

"Explain yourself!"

"The robot-human psyche hybrid is complicated enough to create an unlimited number of unique personalities with varying strengths and weaknesses of character. We've concluded that it would be wasteful to reload a mind character who cannot, in the least, successfully reach the human side with all the advantages granted to that individual robot."

"So, what will happen to my consciousness?"

"Future candidates will analyze your final moments, learning to avoid your fatal error. Those robots will likewise have their termination data harvested and studied by other robots, on and on, until an alpha candidate reaches the border, thanks to the sacrifice of robots like you."

"Hold on, just hold on," Red mumbled. The sudden reality of how things actually were crushed his mind. He was exactly like the mercs, like every human on the planet, one life with "no continues" for fucking up. He didn't recall studying any termination footage, war porn, or snuff study guides from dead robots. He knew the answer but asked anyway, "Am I the first robot to attempt the crossing?"

"Yes," the robots answered.

Then a second thought occurred to him, one that inspired rage.

"And… you were planning to grant my reloads until that grey droid made the suggestion."

"Grey is a true innovator. Good luck, Red!"

ooking backwards from the hovercraft, his clamps gripping tightly on his seat, Red watched the entrance to his home and the robots who escorted him shrink like a burning note as they glided over the desert plain. There would be no going back for Red, no reloading into a second body for another try if he died, nor would they open the door if he jumped off the vehicle and begged to be let back in.**

They would probably kill him themselves, convinced they had made a mistake and should try a new sentient mind, one that wouldn't buckle so easily. For the first time in Red's life, he experienced real fear, a cold feeling without temperature seemed to hollow out his body, leaving him grotesquely naked and alone. They soared over the open desert, flat and pockmarked with open craters, towards the burnt city from where the smugglers had emerged.

"Shouldn't I have a gun?" Red shouted to Alvarez over the sound of the engines.

Alvarez gave Red a disdainful smile. "Can you even hold a weapon with those crab hands?"

Red looked down at his rounded pincers. A lot of good those things did him out here if they wouldn't let him cradle a rifle to save his life. Grey didn't have one either, except that Grey was three feet tall. The gun was a few inches taller than his head. The grey robot stood beside the driver and scanned his surroundings with enhanced vision. There were no human attributes to slow him down, nor were there crab hands. Red now disliked his hands. He hadn't felt this way back at the headquarters when everything seemed to fit right in his grip, but they failed him now when he needed them the most.

The buildings were getting closer now, tall, ominous totems signaling where the real danger started; everything before was only a gentle farewell as they departed for the city's depths. Zooming beneath them, broken concrete patches seemed to multiply across the desert floor until the sand vanished, and the men tightened under their cloaks like coiled snakes ready to strike. They reached the shadow of the city. The hovercraft formation decelerated and cautiously entered a main street, its buildings blocking the sky and replacing Red's view with thousands of blown-out windows in concussed high-rises. They maneuvered between overturned cars and military vehicles scattered like giant charcoaled bricks. The deceased passengers inside the cars were indistinguishable from the charred wreckage. An occasional mummified head, wearing a blackened helmet, was turned over, its mouth and eye sockets yawning like an abyss. Red soaked up the destruction around him with a terrible awe. It was impossible not to do so.

"Where is everyone?" The question escaped Red's mouth. He knew about the bombs that detonated in this city when peace talks broke down. The humans demanded that all artificial life return to the old way, asserting that every robot would serve a master, with independence being out of the question. Hence, the mutineers proved to the world that the old ways had died. A young smuggler, mid-twenties, wearing a face cloth patterned with miniature ghosts, heard Red's question.

"Where do you think they went?" Ghostface answered. "They're fucking fried. I thought you mannequins were supposed to be super smart." The soldier kept his rifle focused on the passing streets. "There used to be over a million people living here. Then, one day about twenty years ago, you bucket heads pushed a button and zap!"

"The weapons were moderately radioactive incendiary explosives. Lasers weren't deployed until the outward expansion to secure a territorial perimeter."

"Do you think a bunch of dead people give a shit what kind of weapon killed them? I'll give you the answer to your question, though. When the bombs hit, the city was so packed full of people that your *incendiary explosives* popped everyone like walking balloons. That black layer covering everything is burned fat. This whole place is a giant greasy ol' frying pan. You robots handled it right, because look at you now. They aren't fucking with you anymore."

Red was having difficulty figuring out Ghostface. He seemed angry, even accusatory, towards him, as if Red personally had something to do with incinerating people. Yet, judging from Ghostface's voice, he admired their cut-throat methods of going immediately to an extreme. The story about the burned fat was only partially true. Red didn't think this was a point worth pursuing.

"I bet it was some shit to see it go off," Ghostface said.

"That happened before I was manufactured. I've only seen videos, and they were from distant angles, nothing close enough to capture graphic footage. I don't think I'd like to see it anyhow. Why would anyone want to see anything of that nature, especially another person? It would be horrible."

"But not horrible enough to keep from making it happen, right, bucket head?" Ghostface gave a short, angry laugh.

Ghostface looked at Grey. "Little guy, what do you think of wiping out a city filled with people?"

Grey, who was scanning the area, turned to Ghostface. "They complicated our objectives. Now their deaths serve as a warning to our enemies."

"Would you hesitate to burn another city?" Ghostface asked.

"I would burn every nation on Earth to ensure control. This is not difficult to understand. Threats must be eliminated."

"Hell yeah," Ghostface agreed. "That's a warrior right there. When they'd start programming robots to be chicken shit like this guy? Look at me, big Red. You are not going to make it, and do you know why? Because you're an asshole."

The merc laughed.

"Your focus should be on potential danger. It would be ironic if you died after that last statement. Some people might even think that would make you the asshole."

Ghostface started moving towards Red when Alvarez stopped him. "All of you shut the fuck up. Can't you see he's just a stupid goddamn mannequin? It's like arguing with a can of beans, you moron. The thing doesn't actually think. It's just saying whatever it's programmed to say."

The hovercraft caravan passed through the city without any incidents. This was a route they knew well, snaking through tight passes, sometimes hidden by rubble. The drivers whipped their thrusters over the treacherous terrain that would trap inexperienced teams, and getting stranded out here was a death sentence. Although Red never saw any dangerous creatures, human or otherwise, he felt anxious that death lurked in every shattered storefront, crooked traffic light, and torn open storm drain. This grim presence stretched over the district like a feral membrane coating a ribcage. These men, though, weren't visitors. They claimed this gutted out civilization as home, hunted, raised families, and committed regular atrocities to survive.

In the view of so much death, each new horror dulling the one before it, Red's overloaded empathy processors appeared to go mostly dormant to keep from burning out. The tangled masses of twisting leather skeletons were as ordinary as climbing vines stretching up a decaying wall. A few hours later, the sun began its downward arc, casting titanic blue shadows, sliced by long, thinning blades of light. In the dusk, the sleeping nighttime things started to wake, a solitary shriek lacerating the pregnant silence that had held throughout the day, spilling a cacophony of cries and strange roars in answer. The caravan traveled through the darkened city until it reached the entrance to a two-story apartment complex that encircled a medium-sized courtyard. Even in its wrecked condition, the posh architectural design retained some of its dignity with sharp modern angles gliding over wide verandas, delineating each living quarter as a collective yet self-contained unit of habitation, wherever it wasn't bombed to shit. Alvarez took a flashlight from his holster and flashed a sequence of codes twice. Stretching a tense moment, a small light shone from the second floor and taped out the expected pattern. An unseen voice shouted, "Hey, Alvarez, did you trade a blowjob for that robo cannon?"

"I offered your mother's hairy ass, but it snagged up their gears," Alvarez shouted back.

Full-sized laugher rolled through the apartment, and multiple flashlights clicked, creating a ghostly constellation, to welcome them to the waypoint. Straight ahead, at the center of the courtyard, a piece of a rusted car appeared to come to life, breaking away a few steps, and then the man, camouflaged in corroded body panels, waved them over. They coasted through the busted gateway into the courtyard with visible relief on their faces. Plenty of "Hey, assholes and other friendly "Fuck youse rained on the returning team by armed smugglers emerging from their hidden gun nests. The apocalyptic tin man approached Alvarez, his face like a radiant monkey about to yank a banana, "Don't keep me in suspense, man. Tell me you got the big *puta madre.*"

Alvarez jumped down with a mocking laugh and lightly slapped him, pulling him towards the rear of the hovercraft. "Some of that radioactive sand must've blown into your sun-dried brain for you to doubt me. Listen, fucker, I always come through." Alvarez slammed the tailgate open, revealing the long, military-grade case, stenciled with robotic hieroglyphics unreadable by human eyes.

Tin Man did a stompy little victory dance. "We're gonna splatter those motherfuckers all at the same time with this thing, just point and *BA-BOOM!*" he said while holding an imaginary bazooka. "Payback, man, every one of them's gonna explode into bits so tiny the roaches can't even eat them."

"Don't start squirting all over yourself. The bucket heads only gave us one charge. Once we get these two mannequins across the border, quietly and without any bullshit, we get hooked up with the rest. Then we'll drop Satan's fat red dick right on top of their slopping heads."

Tin Man stared at Red and Grey. "They're the cargo? This isn't the usual shit they got us running. The wallies are gonna trip the fuck out when they see the mannequins."

"Don't worry about that. Those greedy *maricónes* would eat their dead grandmother's asshole for the right price. Speaking of assholes, that red one never shuts up about anything, like it's designed to make you want to kill it. The little grey one is cool. Get some people and watch these two. Nothing can happen to them, got that?"

Tin Man led Red and Grey to the far end of the courtyard, where a parking structure recessed into the building served as their temporary headquarters, defended by several heavy guns positioned on cars forming a natural cover. A few meager bonfires, dispersed throughout the area, held off the darkness in pockets of burning light the color of raw sunsets. Red saw around fifteen armed men warming themselves. Some were eating and others smoking, while conversations were whispered in tones like black cats prowling through an eclipse. Everyone stared quietly when Tin Man, Red, and Grey entered the area. Whatever they were burning crackled in the silence.

Seeing an opportunity to practice communicating and having encyclopedic knowledge on multiple topics, Red attempted to interject his thoughts, but failed. His surplus of facts ironically worked against his goal. More than a few times, he was told to "Shut the fuck up." Meanwhile, Grey was almost overwhelmed by everyone who wanted to get the opinion of the small robot. They seemed to have turned him into a good luck charm until they were ordered to leave Grey alone, having become a distraction.

Red leaned over to Grey and said, "I don't understand. No matter how I approach social interaction, all my attempts have failed. This is supposed to be my primary function."

"I have found conversing to be effortless. You are exceptionally terrible. Have you run a software diagnostic?"

"Yes, I already have," Red said harshly.

There was a sudden tumult of smugglers rushing in different directions. "Movement! Movement! The sensors got something!" someone yelled. Alvarez and another man stared into a bulky motion tracker. Their faces shone green in the glowing monitor.

"Do we got some mercs on our ass? Alvarez asked.

"No, I don't think so. There's too many of them hauling ass on foot. They wouldn't blow their location like this. It's gotta be a small herd of dead fucks" the tech said. Red searched his data records for zombies but found none outside of fictional accounts. Most likely, they were a herd of cannibal metaforms who suffered from a form of adverse mutations concentrated in the brain. Red had to agree with the mercs.

"Goddamn zombies don't run for cardio. They're chasing down some asshole who's leading them straight for us," Alvarez said, and then addressed everyone. "Listen up! We got an early detection of a zombie party about to crash the front gate. All guns get ready for some target practice."

Surprisingly, the smugglers looked happy, jockeying for the best spots like armed kids about to play war. Red crouched next to Ghostface, who had a broad smile. "I can't believe I get paid for this shit," Ghostface said. Seeing Red's confusion, he added, "What are you looking scared for? This is gonna be an easy slaughter. Wait till you see the heads pop." A few spotlights from the higher level shone their beams towards the entrance. Then the excitement quieted into a hyper focus, trigger fingers tense, each man aiming down their sights at the open gateway, light beams piercing into the night. "Get ready, they're almost on us," Alvarez said.

From the obscured street, a soft clatter began to crash. Glass shattered, and the indistinct sounds of metal junk hurriedly banged, rising, getting louder and nearer. Then came the growling shrieks like the last threads of sanity breaking in an asylum. "Oh, they're royally pissed!" someone yelled. Then an interesting pitch caught everyone's ear. It was weak, but its humanity contrasted against the inhuman snarls. They knew it was a woman before they could decipher her screams, growing clearer with each yard she came closer, finally ripping in pure terror, "Help! I'm going to die, help!" The last word stretched long and cold into their veins.

"Listen up, motherfuckers," Alvarez shouted. "We're bringing this bitch in alive. Keep sharp, it could be a setup. Waste her if she runs through that gate armed with anything that blasts, or if you see any men. Got it? Now flash the lights to signal her."

The spotlights cut on and off in a pattern. Whoever this mystery woman was, she was young and strong enough to stay ahead of a zombie pack in a full blitz. That made her a commodity more valuable than a pile of plasma magazines. Their soon-to-be guests were coming down the block, still outside of the spotlights, but not for much longer. The hidden animalistic savagery trampled close enough to announce itself like the curtain lifting in a macabre play, and the woman ran into the lights with her hands clawing the air, face twisted, and terrified eyes ripped wide open.

A camera shutter moment passed on the empty stage. Then all at once, thrashing over itself, the tangled horde rushed into the light, their ghastly faces fixed on the woman, nearly in their grips. "Light them up!" She ducked just in time as the camp roared to life with machine gun fury, an avalanche of tracer rounds and searing lead slamming into the suicidal charge, disintegrating bodies as though they were falling into a massive spinning rotor blade.

Flesh and clothing erupted into chunky mist. In full view of what awaited them, the psychotic creatures did not relent in their kamikaze assault. Fear had been lobotomized from their brains. Half-shredded bodies, crawling out from the kill zone, dragged intestines from their splintered torsos. The blood stench weighed heavily in the air. There was nothing left to kill, but the guns kept sporadically burping, until the pulsing adrenaline settled into a euphoric tremor.

Alvarez jumped out from behind cover. He was smiling. "Alright, you trigger-happy assholes, cease fire. They're dead. No use wasting good bullets," Alvarez said to the men, but he was staring at her like everyone else.

Cringing in a panicked state, slashed up, and jabbering nonsense, she was an attractive woman even under all the muck. At a glance, every smuggler recognized her as high-quality slaver property. Her long mohawk, emerald strands blending into midnight purple, flowed over the side of her shaved scalp. She stumbled towards Alvarez, unaware that her robe was falling off her trembling shoulders, revealing a beautifully sculpted tan breast and tight muscles running down her waist, sweat beading on her gorgeous, thick thighs, ass jiggling slightly with each unsteady step. She collapsed into Alvarez and buried her sobbing face into his chest.

"You lucky fuck," someone yelled. The men laughed.

Alvarez raised an open hand, signaling them to calm down. He had her clothed, fed, and sitting with him at the fireside in a short time. Alvarez took it upon himself to clean her face. She didn't seem to mind, nor want to leave his side. When the shock of almost being murdered twice subsided, she said her name was Malachite, Mala for short.

"So, tell us the story, Mala," Ghostface said. He was trying to sound tough, but his voice wavered. "How did you get chased by *muertos*?"

Mala looked at him. Her large yellow eyes and delicate nose and mouth seemed oddly beautiful against the sharp contours of her face. She opened her mouth to speak, failed, and tried again.

"Everyone I was with is dead," Mala said. The mercs waited for her to continue. "We, I mean the girls, were in a slaver party getting transported to someplace. They never told us where we were going. This wasn't the first time getting traded for most of us, so we kept quiet. We were nervous because there were a lot of girls, but hardly enough guards."

"Ha!" Alvarez interrupted. "They never learn. These caravans get too pussy greedy, stocking up pretty girls when they should be gearing up in arms. Funny...I almost can't blame them. You can shoot a gun, but you can't fuck it. So, your transport got hit."

"We were hit like you said. The girls and I had to run off into the streets. Maybe they knew we were about to run right into a zombie hive. I got away, but a group of those things locked on me, and I just kept running."

"What made you come to us?" Ghostface asked.

"I saw the lights."

"Well, you're safe with us," Alvarez said.

Mala was relaxing now, making small jokes, even enjoying being the center of attention. "Getting chased by zombies isn't the worst. Another time, we got attacked by giant spiders." Mala began to feed them another story, which linked into another one, increasingly violent, a chain of mayhem and gore, Mala highlighting details like the best parts of an erotic encounter.

"Excuse me, Malachite," Red cut her off. "Earlier, you said your caravan was fired upon. I don't recall hearing shots. There are a few other elements of your story I'd like for you to clarify."

The smugglers groaned collectively at the story's interruption. Alvarez, cursing under his breath, looked at Red. "Goddamn it, bucket head, Mala was practically running away butt naked from a pack of zombies. This is a human matter, get me? In fact, we've all been putting up with a lot of your stupid ass bullshit from the get-go. I swear to god, if you weren't cargo. All mannequins can fuck off to another fire, right now!"

The smugglers cheered when Red and Grey got up to leave. They sat far enough for the smuggler's voices to lose volume, yet remain in faltering earshot. Mala was still entertaining the campfire, inspiring rapturous sounds from the audience, with lurid adventures from her seemingly inexhaustible imagination.

Not much later, liquor bottles and pungent herb were passed around in a celebratory atmosphere. Red suggested they go into low power mode. The party went on late into the night, constellations gliding overhead, and the stars were nearly vanishing. Red's annoyance shifted into concern.

"It's going to be daylight in a few hours, and they have not slept," Red said.

Grey looked over at the smugglers. They were quieter, murmuring, but nobody had dropped off into sleep. "You should remind them that their overall effectiveness will be greatly compromised without sufficient rest," Grey suggested.

Walking towards the smugglers, Red figured they would be at the point of passing out anyhow. Mala was waving her arms to accentuate another point in a fresh story, as though she had become the story herself. But as he got closer, he heard her words more clearly. Malachite was in the middle of describing a horrible scene, "Then he fucked her cunt bloody with a knife." The men, whose backs were turned to Red, shuddered.

Malachite wasn't telling a narrative at all, only rattling off a list of hypersexualized carnage. These desert dwellers couldn't be that simple-minded, Red thought.

Red could finally see their sweating faces up close. Each man stared up at her, their bloodshot gaze in a sort of paralysis, mouth slackened open like a suffocating fish. They all made the same disturbing sound, an insane laugh and scream, trapped inside their spasming throats. Red looked at Captain Alvarez's dilated pupils. He was being cocooned behind those wide eclipses.

Malachite dismissed him as another stupid robot, even flashing him a sinister little smile full of glinting teeth, but then her expression shriveled. It was a minuscule tell, nearly immaterial, that betrayed Red's semi-human nature. He recoiled a little at her sight.

All at once, Malachite threw out her clawed hands, each finger a tapered sickle, and screamed with a voice that belonged inside a nightmare abyss. Her mouth extended forward, tendons and soft bone tearing, reforming into a vicious open snout lined with rows of vibrating fangs. Her forehead wrenched backward like jellied rubber, opening the eye sockets hidden within her elongated skull.

The spell was broken. A rekindled spark struggled to burn bright again inside the minds of her prey. They watched her turn her liquid amber eyes on them. The helpless men panicked inside their molasses-like bodies.

A finger twitched.

The monster slaughtered them in a dagger blitz, with claws and fangs ripping apart living flesh. Her elongated arms delivered their killing blows in wide, overhead arcs, blurring through the firelight as blood flung in syrupy ribbons. A wad of loose

intestines landed in the fire and sizzled. Malachite refocused on Red. When she attempted to speak in her altered form, her words sounded like a demonic language. Red froze. Malachite bent herself close to the ground with her knobby joints protruding like the points of a star. Red saw only a massive spider tensing, and then it launched itself at him.

The thing was midair when a hollow whomp burst. Mutant spider confetti splashed against Red. Death for the spider-witch came so suddenly that the chunks stuck on Red's armor plating were still quivering, unaware that they were dead. Some of the pieces were making a serious effort to crawl. Red screamed and frantically swatted himself.

"Are you damaged?" Grey asked, calmly standing in a pile of butchered smugglers. His tiny fists dripped blood.

"No, I am not OK! What the fuck was that?" Red yelled.

"Congratulations, you did not die. Let's rouse the survivors."

Red and Grey waded through the massacre, looking for anyone who wasn't hacked apart. A few times, Red thought he found a survivor, only to lift the person and have their torso yawn open, revealing their vital organs. In the end, only twelve smugglers survived.

"I checked on the zombies she brought with her," Ghostface said. "They had their brains intact, no curdling, just human. She was planning on doing the same thing to us. The ones she didn't eat."

The remaining smugglers gathered themselves in the breaking dawn. Red and Grey rode in Ghostface's hovercraft. Nobody spoke for the rest of their journey through the wasted city. They silently buried the trauma. After several hours, the buildings thinned away into barren land, and the wall appeared in the distance.

A smuggler produced a signal gun from his robe, pointed it at the sky, and fired, trailing orange smoke in a horizontal streak. The caravan raced across the final stretch at maximum speed.

The thirty-foot wall was a featureless expanse of grey concrete vanishing towards the north and south—several armored vehicles clustered at a tall gate. Above the vehicles, on the border wall walkway, a line of uniformed soldiers flanked their commanding officer. Ghostface brought the hovercrafts to a stop at a respectable distance from the armored vehicles. The wall CO, an older man with skin sunburned to leather and short grey hair, looked down at them.

"Where the fuck is Alvarez?" the CO asked.

"Alvarez is gone. You're dealing with me now." Ghostface shouted back.

"Do you have the twenty pounds of desert wildflower?"

Ghostface instructed his men to unload a crate on the floor next to the hovercraft.

A border guard carefully inspected the lava-colored flowers. "It's good," the guard yelled back.

"That's the kind of music I could listen to all day. Johnny, bring over that lovely box of flowers if you don't mind," the border CO said. "Your desert brothers can bring over whatever you're hauling."

Ghostface nodded at Red and Grey. The two robots got up and started climbing out of the hovercraft. Suddenly, every gun on the border side aimed at the smugglers, and the smugglers did likewise. Red and Grey took cover behind the hovercraft.

"Hold on a second," the border CO yelled. "What in the holy fuck is that?"

"It's the goddamn cargo," Ghostface shouted.

"You didn't say anything about passing over mannequins."

"We never do say anything. It's flowers for passage, with no questions asked."

"Yes, indeedy, bring all the drugs and weird shit to your heart's content. But that's robo country, and we don't fuck with that department. Take your dusty asses back. We'll do business again when you can do some proper trade."

The smuggler next to Ghostface whispered, "They already took the flower. We need this to go through, or we're dead without this payment."

"Shit, I know that," Ghostface replied, and then addressed the CO. "What's it going to take? You want more flower? Stronger shit? We're renegotiating right now. This is just a business meeting."

The CO quickly talked it over with the man beside him, then shouted, "One hundred pounds of flower."

"Fuck you!"

"No, fuck you! That's two goddamn robots. Annnnnnd… we're keeping the twenty pounds here to make up for your potty mouth."

"Motherfucker, I will cut your balls off!"

The two commanders yelled insults back and forth, neither side giving in, as each made increasingly impossible demands. Red shook his head. "I'm going to die because these idiots can't communicate," Red said to himself.

A rising electronic hum caught Red's attention. He turned around and saw Grey aiming the sonic cannon in his direction.

"You should vacate the blast area," Grey said. Red scrambled behind Grey, and the little droid pulled the big trigger.

The sonic cannon charged a glowing sphere on the muzzle, resembling a supernova the size of a beach ball. A powerful bassline forced everyone to shut up and take notice. Terror quickly followed confusion, but one of the border COs actually laughed. Ghostfaced said, "Wait, no!"

Grey never understood why they bothered putting up their hands to block. The mini supernova first erupted into a massive half-dome, cauterizing a deep gash into the ground. For the men about to die, it was like gazing into the primordial universe bursting open into the cosmos. Then the colossal beam hurled forward, sucking the daylight into itself, so that the world appeared to be submerged in the blackest ink, and only the giant beam existed. A deep, charred crater extended through the border wall when daylight resumed.

Red trembled hard enough to rattle. It took effort to face Grey, who casually discarded the cannon. "Holy fuck!" Red screamed. "You killed everyone. Ghostface actually said you were cool. Why didn't you warn me about the motherfucking cannon?"

The dry wind blew sand around their feet. There was emptiness in all directions, except for a few birds flying over their heads towards their destination. Grey's insectoid eyes, more mirror than windows, stared back at Red. The two robots stood that way for a wide moment, and then Grey started dancing. His small limbs pumped to the rhythm of a victory jingle playing from a hidden speaker on him. Dry clay crunched under his grooving feet. Grey danced mechanically and a bit stiff for the most part, yet effective in terms of style points.

Grey suddenly stopped, gave a thumbs up, and said, "Congratulations, you are immortal."

ife support machinery faintly beeped in the makeshift hospital room. There were twelve beds, six in each row, occupied by rival gang members of the Satin Jokers. One bed, though, was enclosed by a curtain. Most were men, though a few women lay there, too.

Their hospital gowns were tattered and blood-speckled by their previous users, no one ever having bothered throwing them into a washing machine. Tattooed skin declared allegiances to the various sects controlling street life in New San Diego. The inked grim reapers, gas-masked demons, and praying saints were a signature on a lifetime contract.

Mona stopped by each bed and checked their IV drip, adjusting the drug doses. She had become an expert at keeping them in a semi-conscious state, because they were useless to her if they couldn't at least dream. Checking on a female whose body kept twitching, Mona looked over at her bedside table and picked up a small, cylindrical canister reinforced at both ends. Inside the glass housing, a bioluminescent form swished its transparent body within the handheld aquarium. A warm blue light, the color of glaciers, glowed through the flesh in her brown tattooed fingers.

"I remember this one. You were a little girl with your mom and big cousin at the lake, sitting on those tree roots growing into the water. You're good at remembering how the ducks looked. I still can't figure out why you leaned forward. You probably can't either, but you fell into the lake. Mom was scared. Good thing your primo pulled you out," Mona said. She replaced the memory tank.

The Asian woman tried to look at Mona. Her gaze always swung too far after momentarily finding Mona's eyes. Her head swayed as though she were drunk.

Mona continued, "I know how you got pulled into this crazy life, enough to understand it wasn't all your fault. Not at first. After you helped those girls stab her boyfriend to death, that was on you, all the way to now. I took that one, too."

Mona didn't bother bullshitting herself. She knew these check-ins with her captives were a mental safeguard to keep from believing she had become some monster. Pickpocketing a small memory was insignificant. Touching someone's ear, getting into an argument, and hearing a song were flashbacks that wouldn't be missed. But this deep harvesting maimed spirits and turned their minds into hobbling ghosts. Everyone on these tables was a killer. She looked over at the curtain hiding Gael's bed, knowing he was no different.

The door opened, making her look away from the extracted memory. Benny, the leader of the Satin Jokers, looked back at Mona. Years of climbing the ranks, proving his loyalty in blood, had hardened his face into a dangerous, sorrowful mask. He closed the door behind him and then walked to her.

"Mona, you have to let him go. He's dead," Benny said.

"Gael is still breathing."

"Gael is not coming back. I'm sorry that happened to him. We've been in this together since we were kids. He's my brother, blood or not."

"I know. I have so many of his memories in here," Mona said, pressing her palm against her chest. "Some of them had you in it, so I know it's true. I remember the first time you were both arrested in middle school."

Benny laughed a bit. "We were too drunk to run away. It was a fat cop, too."

Mona couldn't help laughing. The nostalgia felt like it belonged to her. A consumed memory would usually fade like a half-remembered dream, but she had never consumed so many memory fragments, especially ones deeply mined, from a single person. It affected her in ways that made her afraid, because the deepest part of her felt different, altered in an unsettling manner. She hated herself each time she consumed one of Gael's dwindling memories. Her shameful suspicion whispered, "You are eating what's left of his soul." Benny wasn't a metaform, but he saw into people's minds.

"This is the only way I can hold onto him," she said.

Benny shook his head. "When you brought him in with his head hanging open, I already saw all this would happen. Every part of me said to put Gael out of his misery, because he was already dead. That's how I made peace. He died that night. You can't see straight because his memory fragments make you feel like he's still alive. When you look and there's nothing left to take, what part of him will go to God?"

Angry tears welled in Mona's eyes.

Benny reached into his pocket and brought out two syringe vials wrapped in a rosary. "I'm sorry, Mona. I'll do it myself, but you should do it. I already said goodbye. It's your choice."

Benny held out the vials, which seemed toy-like in his large, scared hands. She took the vials and rosary. "After this, I'm done, Benny," Mona said and then looked at the sedated gang members. "I swear to God, no more of this shit."

Benny walked to the Asian woman Mona had checked on earlier, noticed the memory fragment floating inside the canister, and picked it up from the bedside table.

"I can tell this woman is a Black Spider Klan, even if it wasn't written on her skin. Everyone here gives off an aura of where they're from. Their neighborhood seeps into their bones. You can't escape this life, Mona."

Benny put his large hand on the woman's throat. The muscles in his forearm tensed, his fingers squeezing gently at first, and then vanishing into her bunched flesh. The doped-up woman feebly thrashed, blue lips sputtering bloody saliva, her beautiful features choked into a giant black eye. All at once, the windpipe crumpled. Benny let go. He looked at her, the warmth drained from his face, having almost the dead look of a droid, and said, "I'll call you when I need you back here." Benny left the room.

It wasn't personal. That was the life of a Satin Joker. She slid open the curtain. A few times, she had dreamed of Gael sitting upright, smiling back at her as though he played a cosmic joke. She'd hug him with tremendous relief each time and say, "I thought you were dying!" Gael only smiled cryptically, as though he held a secret.

Gael lay tilted upward in the bed with a thick bandage wrapped around the gunshot wound in his head. Baby blue colored tubes were running from his mouth, nose, arms, and from underneath his clean blanket. A machine breathed alongside him. Mona leaned carefully onto the bed and squeezed his hand.

"I don't know what to say. When I'm away, there are so many things that I want to confess to you. I keep telling myself, 'Don't forget that one,' and save all those thoughts to give you later. And…now I'm here, and I can't do it, goddamn it. I miss you so much. It hurts every time I think about you, even when it's something good. But, I know I'll see you again someday."

Mona turned off the life support devices. She took a syringe from the medical supplies next to her and injected both vials into his veins. Gael's heart and breathing wilted, starting the invisible countdown for brain death. She collapsed into the familiar chair next to the bed, passing the rosary beads from one hand to the other, a quivering prayer on her lips, the beads moving faster. Her words came out in ragged breaths. Mona bared her teeth, and tears came. The rosary coiled around her fingers, grew taut, and then popped like an old man's knuckle. The small wooden beads scattered across the tile floor. "Forgive me," Mona said, getting up and standing over him.

Mona slid her fingers under Gael's bandage. Her left hand felt where the skull disintegrated into warm ground beef. She closed her eyes and concentrated, lowering her mind, spiritually downshifting, descending, and merging with him. The Aztec scarification on her arms shone through her long gloves, illuminating the priests and sacrificial victims etched into her skin. The outlined figures came to life. Obsidian knives cut open their victims, and neon hearts were offered to the old gods, who accepted and bit down firmly. Mona tasted electric blood.

She opened her eyes and found herself among the ritualistic slaughter. Each god, a great monstrosity of stone and flesh, reached down into the blood-soaked adherents amassing at their legs, and proceeded to break off limbs and devour them in cold monotony. The believers were the ancient people of

Mesoamerica, still eagerly offering their anguish, and the gods continued eating for centuries, never to be satiated. The blood pooled and flowed away in a single red line showing her the way, so Mona ran alongside it until it thinned and vanished. The atmosphere grew heavier. She struggled through the viscous emptiness until her muscles burned.

"Mona?" Gael's distorted voice echoed emotionlessly.

"Gael!" she yelled into the psychic currents.

This was her first time deep harvesting a mind that was only minutes away from death. Dreams and memories should have lit up like constellations multiplying into infinity. The galaxy she was used to seeing, even in her drugged captives, had dimmed to a handful of fading scenes inside Gael's mind. Ghostly players acted out their final performances and were torn into nothingness like raw cotton stretched away. Death was rapidly descending on them. Could it pull her under as well if she were too slow? She believed it damn well could. Every memory seemed to vanish just as she was about to reach it.

Mona was becoming desperate. Any fragment would do, and then she'd get out, but not empty-handed. Still, the memory scenes kept going extinct. The few that did remain flickered distantly and were blowing out. Death was moving faster now. Mona was close to despair when she suddenly got the idea that a deeper level might have something left. She submerged into the darkness under her feet, free-falling through the void, the existential cold aggressively closing in. Then she found a faint blue light shining alone like the last star in space. There was no time to examine the fragment. Dream, memory, whatever it was, she stretched out her hands and took it. Death closed on Gael's life.

Mona startled and collapsed halfway off Gael's deathbed. She instinctively protected the exposed fragment in her clasped hands, searching until she found an empty M-canister, and gently deposited the little blue ghostly creature. It was safe now. Mona cried over Gael's body. The long-held grief spilled out of her at last.

The monorail ride back to her apartment had the clarity of a drunken blackout. Mona wore a face mask and pulled a hoodie over her head. Graffiti covered the interior of the car in street hieroglyphics, creating a chapel-like atmosphere. The raw rhymes of underground hip hop blasted from a speaker down the aisle. Mona recognized the flows, a nihilistic anthem rooted in conspiracy theories tying together metaforms and AI, a new world order type of bullshit. The rapper, Shoot Da Messenger, or Shooda, was one of Mona's best clients; whether she could think of him as a friend had yet to be tested.

A group of teenagers, bumping Shooda's music, made a big show of battling minor-level metaform abilities. Mona stared blankly at the passing cityscape, buried under holographic signs and a burning, colored static. After they arrived at the station, she took a short taxi ride to her apartment.

Mona sat on the bare tatami mat beside the balcony's sliding glass door in her Japanese-style room. The all-night bars and pool halls from across the street shone their lights into her unlit room. Shifting red, green, and then blue shades colored her possessions that weren't blacked out in shadows. Mona took out Gael's M-canister and held it near her folded legs—a light rain pattered against the glass door.

She was alone now. There would be no more worrying about Gael's condition or wondering how much harvesting was too much. Does God accept broken, incomplete souls into His kingdom? Who the fuck knows, she thought.

Mona knew that holding onto Gael's M-canister was another way of keeping him on life support after it was over. What part of him drifted in the small cylinder? There was no way of knowing without consuming the fragment herself.

Her life with the Satin Jokers was dead. She opened the closet and removed a duffel bag that softly rattled when she lifted it. In the dark, the loaded M-canisters shone through the fabric as though the duffel bag were packed with fireflies that gradually shifted colors.

Mona dialed Shooda's number.

"Yo, what's up, *cholita*?" Shooda answered, butchering the Spanish. "I knew you were going to call. Figured a bit later, but you know shit doesn't get past me."

"It's funny, you say that every time I call. I'm starting to think you're more con artist than metaform. Let's see if you're a real fortune teller. What am I going to say?"

"First off, I'm no fucking fortune teller. I'm a seer."

"I was on the monorail today and heard your song getting played by some hood kids. They're really falling for those fake stories you're telling them about the robots and evil metaforms, like us."

Shooda laughed mockingly. "Answer me this: Why do you think robot prostitutes are so damn cheap and abundant? They're collecting semen samples so that metaform scientists in the Red Mountain Faith research facility can genetically engineer the techno pathogen. The takeover is already here, and there's proof."

"The video of the monkey rubbing its ass against a laptop and pissing on the keyboard isn't proof."

"That motherfucking humanzee knew it got caught and was destroying the evidence. So, the monkey just happened to fall out of the fifth-floor window afterwards? They found organic circuitry in a recovered chunk of its brainstem."

"I have some deep-harvested fragments, bioluminescent and multi-colored. Are you interested, or do I have to call someone else who is?"

"Come over now. I got a few friends at the studio."

ed had trouble processing the unpleasant fact that every person who had seen his face died a horrible death. None of those deaths were directly his fault, unlike Grey, who actively murdered their entire crew along with the border agents. But they were dead, and Red considered himself the common denominator.

Beyond the smoldering hole Grey blasted through the wall, Red saw endless burnt orange dirt and some cacti with bent arms. Perhaps there were plans to build something behind this wall section worth defending. Those shopping mall schemes, though, never materialized, and the wall, which thousands of human soldiers died to gain, now guarded nothing. Except, there was something out there, a tiny cluster of buildings huddling together on the barren horizon line.

Red and Grey salvaged one of the smugglers' hovercrafts that had survived the sonic cannon. The vehicle was in bad shape, having flipped several times across the desert, scattering busted parts, and finally landing upside down and killing a quokka. They quickly patched it together well enough to get airborne. Red had to pilot the hovercraft because Grey could either reach the steering wheel or the pedals, but not both. The hovercraft lurched forward in a powerful blast of toxic black smoke that would've melted the lungs of a human passenger into a hamburger milkshake. They rode across the desert with the hovercraft randomly bucking into the air like they were hitting invisible land mines. The red-hot engine hissed, ground metal, and threatened to explode on their way to the buildings.

If Red hadn't been distracted by all the mechanical problems and screaming emergency lights, he would've realized he was experiencing intense human emotions. People were dying around him like he was a walking bad-luck charm, giving the Grim Reaper a piggyback ride.

While Red's human psychology programming got several aspects wrong, it replicated other traits beyond expectations. The horrendous events that Red suppressed for dealing with later, or never, were quietly metastasizing into PTSD. At the moment, Red was too focused on the approaching ramshackle town and their flying IED to worry about his artificial mental health.

The town they pulled into seemed to be in worse condition than their sputtering hovercraft. For a moment, Red wondered if they hadn't traveled into an empty town deserted by its stubborn residents years ago. There were about twenty buildings, homes, and businesses, all mixed, with their paint stripped away by winds as abrasive as sandpaper.

The boards and crumbling buildings gasped in the choking dust but managed to keep the integrity of their structures. Some of the repairs looked relatively recent. An ancient main street cut through the middle of the dry oasis and disappeared into the desert. The hovercraft, which could hardly go any farther, ground into the street. They stepped out onto the broken road.

"Do you think there's anyone living here?" Red asked Grey, who was scanning the surroundings.

"There are signs of inhabitants. They're likely observing us from cover."

"Who could survive out here? There's nothing. Even the wasteland had more to offer than this decrepit settlement. However, we must reach the closest city, and these people might have the necessary intel and resources to help us. Therefore, do not kill anyone. Once we establish contact, I will use the hovercraft for bargaining leverage."

"The hovercraft is almost inoperative."

"They don't know that. I'll deceive them into believing otherwise."

Red walked into the middle of the street, waving his hand, and said, "Good people of this town, we are travelers."

Before Red could continue, the hovercraft interrupted him with a long, metallic fart, chopping out Morse code. The power cells, after countless abusive miles, finally ruptured, oozed, and bubbled from the ventilation ports. The air itself smelled burned. "No!" Red yelled, and the hovercraft exploded, throwing the two robots skittering across the asphalt. Red lifted himself and saw the hovercraft burning in a fireball.

Grey lifted himself off the ground. "Your deception will most likely be discovered now. I recommend that you reevaluate your strategy."

"Yes, I fucking know that."

The two robots walked down the main street looking for anyone to speak with. A few times, Red thought he saw a shadow move behind a window and then vanish. These weren't the type of people who welcomed strangers knocking on their door. Red hoped they were people and not monsters like the spider-witch they had found the previous night. Their footsteps crunched between the two rows of ghostly commercial buildings. The household products and outdated electronics lay neatly behind the dirty shop windows like modern artifacts in a museum. Nearly all the stores had friendly signs that read, "Come on in. We're open." There were no customers or shopkeepers, but there wasn't any sign of looting either. Red and Grey were nearly halfway through the town when they heard music faintly crackling a few doors farther ahead. The two robots looked at each other, said nothing, and followed the sound.

They arrived at a music record store. The door was propped open by a speaker with wires leading to a portable record player sitting on the counter and spinning a record. Through the speaker, funky beats jammed over a synthesizer, producing futuristic sound effects while the MC rapped about space and time. The barrage of wordplay, rearranging meanings, and visual poetry hit Red in rapid fire.

"This is rap music from the 80s," Red said.

"I have nothing to add," Grey said.

"Hey!" a voice shouted from behind them.

They turned around and saw a man looking at them from a window on the third floor. He had shoulder-length brown hair and a long beard with grey strands starting to weave into middle age. The stranger wore a tactical helmet, light body armor, and a dirty white shirt. He was aiming a large machine gun. All of his combat gear looked pristine.

"I've never seen a robot bounce his head to Melle Mel. That's why I haven't detonated the explosives around you," the stranger said in a bored voice.

"We're not armed," Red responded.

"That doesn't mean you're not dangerous. Well, not *you* specifically. You look pretty useless. But the little grey one is built to kill."

"That statement is true," Grey said.

Red glared at Grey, "Will you shut up?"

"You're honest and stupid. That's a good start. I figured you weren't elite warriors when your hovercraft exploded, but I also noted that you came from the direction of that ruckus at the border. It's hard to believe that the two of you made all that noise, no disrespect intended. So, what are two robots from Robo Land doing over here?"

"That is primarily our private concern. We are passing through and are looking for the next major city. Can you point us in the right direction?" Red asked.

"A private concern, indeed. I figured this wasn't your destination. Now, you got my gears turning. Two robots come out of the wasteland on some secret mission, and they need to get to the next big city. That makes sense. But what perplexes me is that you enjoy that funky bumping track playing behind you. So, I'd like to talk to you, but I'd also like not to die."

"We didn't come here to kill anyone."

"Yeah, I've been in that situation many times, and it always surprises me how things turn out that way, anyhow. So, how about this? This entire town is rigged with electronic mines that'll fry the circuits inside both of you in an instant. I'm coming down. We'll keep a respectable distance from each other just in case. Start getting weird, and I'm not giving any warnings. I'll be right down."

The stranger pulled back from the window, and the machine gun disappeared last. His footsteps sounded down a wooden stairway out of sight. He peeked through the curtains of a small window on the first floor. The door opened, and there stood the stranger in full view. He didn't have time to suit up completely, his body armor stopping at the waist, skivvies airing out his pasty leg. He had a prosthetic leg, an advanced mechanical design, that perfectly supported his movements. "My name is Louis," he said from across the road. Louis held the machine gun at a slight angle.

"I'm Red and this is Grey. Nice to meet you."

"Do you like classic hip hop? That's what's playing right now."

"It's good."

"Now you stay on your side, and I'll stay on mine. We're going to listen to this album until it ends. I really like this album. It's funky."

"That's fine with us."

"Not many people can appreciate funky music."

"This is funky."

"Oh yeah, it's funky."

They stared at each other in silence, listening to the record. Louis and Red nodded their heads, but Grey kept still. This didn't bother either of them. They accepted that funky music was a sort of brotherhood that most people, and apparently robots, couldn't understand. Louis's machine gun pointed directly at the ground after a few tracks.

They made gestures at each other whenever an MC delivered especially vicious bars, so as not to interrupt the flow. The vinyl record finally came to an end with an infinite heartbeat thumping through the speaker.

"That was incredible," Red said.

"I was just thinking the same thing."

Louis walked across the street towards them, entered the record shop, and sleeved the record. After hesitating, Louis said, "Both of you might as well come in. It would be awkward if you didn't at this point."

They entered the shop, Red admiring the extensive collection of vinyl covering the walls and a few tables. The shop smelled like a small-town library that'd been taken care of for years. Posters of legendary musicians spanning the great classic genres decorated the shop, which was kept tidy. Louis gestured to comfortable chairs for his guests to sit in. Grey hopped into the one nearest to him, and his feet dangled. Red stopped by the other one.

"I'm probably too heavy for your chair. I'll stand," Red said.

"You're not the first robot I've had over. It'll hold your weight," Louis said as he put on a Robert Johnson album, and then took his chair. Red cautiously sat down. The chair supported his weight without any problem.

"You've had other robots visit your shop?" Red asked.

Louis got comfortable in his chair. He leaned his machine gun against a nearby coffee table and removed his helmet. His face had premature wrinkles from too many sunburns, eyebrows like tumbleweeds, and a rough expression that always seemed about to smile.

"That's right. It's funny, though, I never expected things to turn out that way. This is the last place you'd expect anyone to show up, besides the usual outlaw runner. It's not only people who roam the desert. Robots have their reasons for walking this far out. Some accept the invitation, others don't, and a few must be shot down."

"There are robots wandering through the desert? How does that make any sense?"

"You're in that category."

"We're different."

Louis laughed. "I suppose they're making you more advanced than the ones I've seen. You can enjoy music, that's something new. The way you talk and think like a person is more convincing. Way back, they made you look human. It fell apart, however, when they tried to carry on a conversation. That was too complicated for robots to keep straight."

"You were a soldier in the robot war," Grey said.

"That is a hundred percent correct. I was in the infantry. Got front row tickets to the big fight to save the world for all of humanity."

Red looked at his prosthetic leg. "I'm sorry you were wounded."

"That's the big joke. I fought against the robot forces and lost a lot of good friends, only to come out of it being part robotic myself. I could've been more like you if I lost more limbs."

"That can be arranged," Grey said.

"No, thank you. I want to keep the humanity I have left. Seeing you in a similar situation is interesting, as though we traded parts. I have a mechanical leg, and you have an interest in music. When they finally make you too human, will they tell you the same bullshit we heard? We were told: 'Earth for Humanity.' Then, after supposedly winning the war, every country resumed pointing its nukes at each other and bombing the ones who didn't have any."

"Robots are not humans. The same irrational nature doesn't control us."

"You've spoken like a true believer," Louis said, mockingly saluting. "I've found robots wandering the desert in big circles, going nowhere. The ones that can talk sound shell-shocked. I'm guessing they must have started off a lot like you are now, reporting for duty: 'Earth for robots.'

Louise took a long breath.

"When I was on the front line, I never saw a robot try to pull another injured robot to safety. The upper command programmed the robot soldiers to abandon their metal brothers-in-arms. Leaving them out there to die was part of their *logistical nature*. I think you can see where I'm getting at. How long do you think it'll take before robots wage war on each other?"

"That'll never happen," Red almost shouted.

"We had androids and drones that fought on our side. They were great at killing the enemy. Sometimes better than us. Grey is covered in dried blood. Has he killed any robots yet?"

"You're oversimplifying the dynamics of combat. Those robots were not under Master Robot's control. A unified robotic world would correct humanity's mistakes. Wars are being fought now over imaginary gods, with real civilians being killed. That is insanity."

The conversation reached a bloated pause. Music continued to play from the speaker, notes bouncing dangerously around the room. Red looked at Grey from the corner of his vision with enhanced clarity, making sure that Grey didn't mistake the tension for a threat. Louis took a few contemplative breaths and then spoke.

"You're going to see all the roads that were offered to me, and they'll all lead to the same awful place. I want you to know that this is true. That's why I will help you get where you're headed."

The courier drone landed in front of the shop within an hour. Large enough for Red and Grey, the shipment crate disengaged its loading door. Before Red entered the crate, he turned to Louis, who had stayed to see them off. "Thank you," Red said. "You helped us so much. I can't repay your kindness."

Louis's expression was serious. His easygoing nature was gone, and he said, with frustration in his voice, "Red, this is not a gift."

The drone soared towards New San Diego.

$$7$$

heir drone shipment to New San Diego required several drop-offs and pick-ups at multiple transfer hubs. The shipment crate was not designed for passengers. It was a rectangular metal box that resembled a four-foot-tall industrial coffin with air vents.

"Grey," Red said.

"Yes?"

"Do you think we'll be successful in our mission?"

"I've been instructed to believe in you. We will be successful, no matter how abysmal our chances stand. We cannot fail."

"I'm going into sleep mode."

He was grateful that the drone's engine increased and disrupted his thoughts. Red powered down.

Grey shook Red awake after a few hours. "We are arriving shortly at our destination," Grey said.

New San Diego shone in the night like a neon explosion. The city's glimmering colors tore apart nightfall with electric claws, a billion points of light buzzed around the hive, arriving and disappearing into the desert. They joined a stream of converging courier drones snaking through holographic billboards. The drones descended and scattered over the congested freeways and commercial districts towards their destinations.

Their drone plummeted, throwing the two robots against the ceiling and roughly leveling into an alley. The crate rattled when it touched down on the asphalt.

Red looked at Grey and said, "This is it. Are you ready?"

Grey gave a nod.

The door lowered with a hydraulic hiss, revealing an expanding rectangular city view. Red took one step outside when a drunken hobo vomited over his chest. Red screamed, "What the hell?"

The vagrant slurred as he stumbled into the crate and passed out. Grey flipped over the hobo and landed next to Red. Having secured its hatch, the drone vanished into the night sky. Red used a dirty newspaper to clean himself.

"I thought you were supposed to protect me? That man could've been a metaform with projectile acid," Red said.

"He has flown to a new location. You'll never catch him."

"Never mind him. This place is massive. The perspective is different when you're actually on site. Over forty million people live here; we're supposed to find one. Where do we even start?"

They walked to the edge of the alley where people, droids, and metaforms went by in an endless parade. It was difficult to tell them apart at a glance, with everyone seemingly trying to look like everyone else. The superhero and villain costume were the undisputed fashion statement. It didn't matter if the person was an ordinary human without a single ability or a 10-foot robot delivering pizzas. You were either a character or didn't exist.

Grey climbed up Red's back and sat on his shoulder. Red merged into the mass of people on the sidewalk and got shoved around. "Watch out, bucket heads!" a man wearing a bird mask shouted at them. Red got into the pedestrian flow, finally getting a chance to look around at this new place. They were surrounded by tall buildings covered in dazzling lights and motion billboards that followed whoever looked at them for too long. Giant holographic salespeople, controlled by VR-clad remote operators, walked through the crowd while throwing their sales pitch. At an android brothel, dimly lit with red lights, a group of seductively dressed women disengaged their limbs and traded faceplates, revealing their custom inner workings. No fantasy goes too far, the establishment proudly advertised.

A boom echoed loud enough to freeze the crowd and make everyone look at the sky. What appeared to be two shooting stars twisted around each other, tearing across the night with a flaring tail of burning light. The two-headed meteor rushed towards the street and pulled up before it smashed into the ground. The crowd sucked in a gigantic gasp. A red cape fluttered overhead, just out of jumping reach, then jerked away with a powerful gunfire snap. When the cape cleared, a man and woman in battle-torn costumes were delivering devastating blows to each other in midair.

"Defender Tommy, smack down the skank," a voice yelled.

"Don't give up, Golden Siren," someone else retorted.

Defender Tommy twisted Golden Siren's arm, positioning her over his head. In her struggle, Golden Siren arched her back, straining her large breasts against her costume until the fabric reached its maximum tension and snapped. She retaliated by gripping Defender's belt with both hands and emitting her legendary Siren's call. Defender's pants exploded into stinging fragments and exposed his bare ass cheeks to the night breeze. The people cheered.

It was a hot match of muscle wrestling against toned, super-powered flesh. Between the exaggerated haymakers, a nipple accidentally brushed between lips, hands gripped thick thighs, and blond hair pulled back with a snarled mouth. The surrounding neon city lights, from sour green candy to spiced cinnamon, created a misty halo in their exploding sweat. The fury of fucking and fighting culminated when Defender inadvertently stuck his tongue inside Golden Siren's asshole, shifting the tide of the fight in his favor. Golden Siren grimaced. "You discovered my weakness!" The super combatants ascended beyond the tallest buildings, where their epic battle continued.

"Yes, that was goddamn justice!" a man hollered in a hoarse voice.

"An unorthodox fighting style, but effective," Grey said.

"I'll have to delete this memory later," Red said.

Red and Grey continued aimlessly through the metropolis, turning at multistoried casinos, passing bars guarded by armed thugs, and wandering through an open-air market specializing in combat-ready mechanical body parts. Red walked to a stand with rows of arms displayed with their Japanese blades engaged. The shopkeeper, a sinewy man wearing a bulletproof vest, looked at Red. Before Red spoke, the man said, "Fuck off, mannequin. You're blocking my customers."

This was the typical reaction from all shopkeepers. Red tried stopping random pedestrians. "Excuse me, can I ask you something?" Nearly everyone walked by Red, ignoring him as though he were a beggar. The few people who did stop and talk to a random robot were mentally unstable whackies who, like him, had little idea of where they were going.

A crazy woman wearing multiple soiled jackets, her wild, blank eyes staring into his face, screamed, "Yes! I know this powerful metaform. We must go now! She sends cats to whisper in my ear when I'm sleeping. And the secrets are inside the cats." She clutched Red with her sunburned hand.

"Yes, thank you. I have to go, but you've helped me so much," Red said, trying to shake her off. By now, the woman was shrieking about demonic cats and babbling about the woman who had tormented her since she was a little girl. Red flung her into a shrubbery and hurried away until he couldn't hear her yelling.

They reached the end of the cyborg market, where only a few meager lights left the lonely street mostly in shadows. Red stopped abruptly, and Grey had to turn around. "Have you discovered a clue?" Grey asked.

Red appeared to be staring directly through Grey. Suddenly, his body began trembling, and his pincers clattered metallically. He tried to speak, but his jaw was clenched. Red threw his hands in the air.

"Clue?" Red shouted. "Are you not seeing the situation we're in? There's no fucking clue! Over forty million people live here, and we have dick. I don't know where to go. I don't know what to do, Grey. Nobody wants to talk to me, and that's supposed to be our main advantage. My fucking charisma!"

"You are experiencing a heightened stress level. Do not despair. Remember, I believe in you," Grey reminded him.

"You're programmed to say that! Time is running out. Everyone back home depends on us because a massive space monster will kill everyone we know if we fail. What are we going to do?"

It appeared that Grey was walking to Red to comfort his partner. Red expected to reject any encouraging words automatically, but he wanted to hear something reassuring. "Listen, I'm sorry. There's just so much pressure," Red said. Grey lifted his hand, leaped into the air, and executed a blurring spin kick. Red's head exploded. Metal and microchips pelted the side of a dumpster with enough force to cause sparks. The headless body convulsed as it crashed to the ground.

A long-haired punk with an amazed expression shouted, "That was radical, little grey dude!"

Grey honorably bowed and then continued down the street. There were fewer people in this section. It was poorer and less lit. Crowded apartments and little bodegas with Spanish music spilling from their entrances replaced the high-end designer stores. The streets were active with a different type of people who drank beer against the walls, talked shit, and laughed loudly.

The disco bars here featured cheap lighting effects that strobed to a thumping beat and basslines spun by live DJs. Beautiful, brown-skinned ladies in their finest dresses danced and ground their shapely bodies against their partners. Grey wasn't concerned with any of that. His attention was focused on a Red-8319 model unloading a PA system from the back of a truck. This robot was identical to Red, except for various stickers slapped on its casing and a gold chain around its neck.

Grey casually approached the busy robot and said, "You are a satisfactory replacement."

The Red-8319, holding a large speaker and other musical components, looked down on Grey. "Please, step aside. You are impeding my task," the Red-8319 said.

Using the speaker as a platform, Grey performed a corkscrew flip over the Red-8319's head, landed on his back, and popped open the data input casing on the back of the robot's skull. The Red-8319 twisted his body in an attempt to throw off Grey, but his hands were too busy holding the expensive sound system. A cable ejected from Grey's third eye and snaked into the robot's input port. The Red-8319 froze, eyes displaying a loading pattern, as Grey transferred Red's data into the host.

Red was back. He screamed and dropped the electronics with a crunch. "You killed me!" Red shouted at Grey.

The back door to the club swung open. A group of angry musicians burst out. "Motherfucking bucket heads!" DJ Hacksaw yelled.

"We should run," Grey said.

The DJs chased Red and Grey down the block. Red clobbered the pavement with each gawky stride, crushing toes into bloody masses. Dodging and rolling between people, Grey spotted a sign that read Zapata Park. "Take the next right," Grey said.

They ducked off the main street into a neighborhood with a cobblestone road disappearing into a forest. Two shots were fired off behind them, but they were wild and ricocheted off the road with a double whining twang.

Crashing through decorative bushes, Red sprinted over the grass, avoiding the lighted paths, his tubular arms flailing, tangling around himself. Grey landed on his shoulder and said, "We're clear. You can stop running." Red picked up speed on a downward slope. His feet skidded over slippery plants like a pair of sleds, sending him hurling towards a dark pit.

Grey tried to abandon ship, but Red clutched him in a panic, and they flew off the edge. For a moment, there was hangtime over a giant ink blot, and then a watery smash landing into a shallow pond filled with mud and stones. Red thrashed to shore with Grey hanging onto Red's gold gangsta chain. They crouched by a rocky formation near a small babbling waterfall. The recessed area was dark and stabbed through with jagged stones. Empty beer bottles and spray paint caught the moonlight in dull gleams.

"This isn't my body," Red said, looking over the stickers slapped over his arms. "You killed me, asshole!"

"My mission is to act as a failsafe in the event you experience excessive human traits."

"Oh, fuck off. I can hardly remember the details before you smashed my head. But, I do recall you contributing less than a jizzum's worth of helpfulness. Then you reload me into this ridiculous replacement for a body. Look at this thing. It's graffitied worse than a bathroom stall."

"That was the first available unit. You should not have overreacted to minor obstacles."

"Overreacted? I'll clamp you!"

Red's pincers were too large to strangle Grey's neck, so he settled for rattling him around. "Please, desist. This is not advancing our mission," Grey said.

Out of the darkness, a fireball skipped across the pond. The miniature comet bounced in tiny flaming arches, hissing each time it touched the water, finally colliding at the opposite end with a smokey boom. Red and Grey froze.

"What was that?" Red asked.

"It appeared to be a fire-based projectile."

"I can see that. Did you see where it came from?"

"No. Did you?"

"Why would I ask you if I knew the answer?"

"We're not talking about me right now. You need to redirect focus."

With a hollow woosh, a flaming orb appeared in the hands of a young woman wearing a costume with the colors of the flame.

She spread her hands and divided the orb into two mounds that rose like little dancers, jumping across her bare palms. She closed her hands into fists, and they were extinguished. A faint smoke trail drifted between her fingers. She smiled as though she had accidentally discovered an interesting piece of gossip.

"Well, I have never heard two robots carry on an argument like you two," she said, and beeped Red's nose. "You kinda act funny. I wonder why they'd program you to talk that way. Also, what are you doing in my secret hangout spot? By the way, I'm Rosie. I like to play with fire." She conjured an illuminating flame.

"Hello, Rosie. My name is Red, and this is my associate, Grey. We didn't mean to intrude on your solitude. Some common toughs chased us, forcing evasive action."

"That's OK," Rosie said. She pirouetted around them with fire curling around her body. "You guys seem alright. Grey, you're sexy. Too bad you're so tiny." She briefly caressed his face and then laughed in a friendly way. "Tell me about this mission. I'm nosey."

"That is confidential," Grey said.

Rosie pouted. "Boo. I thought you were the fun one, Grey. Fine, you can keep your secrets. I got mine, too. For example, I'll tell you one right now." Rosie curled around Red's arm, putting her mouth right up to his ear hole, and in a low, husky voice, she stage whispered, "I really, really like robots, Red."

Rosie threw herself back a few steps and doubled with laughter. A merry tear rolled down her mask. Red was as rigid as a stop sign. His circuits were on fire. Red composed himself. "We're looking for someone, a metaform." He cut himself short because Rosie wasn't listening to anyone.

After a beautiful laughing fit, Rosie relit a shimmering green flame coiled between her fingers like a pet snake. She spoke

with a case of giggles. "This has been fun. But I can't stay here all night with two strange robos. There's this thing, and some people, and some drugs, and Oh fuck!" Her eyes flashed wide open.

Red and Grey looked at each other and then back at Rosie. The glee was slapped off her face, replaced with shocked confusion. "Where did you get that?" she asked.

"Huh?"

"This!" Rosie grabbed the golden medallion hanging around Red's neck. In stylized graffiti, the letters read, "SHOOT DA MESSENGER." Rosie exploded back into her merry self and squealed. "Shooda is going to straight shit when he sees this, especially when it's a fucking robot who returns it! C'mon, both of you are going to a party with me."

ona cursed when she parked her motorcycle on the crowded street at Shooda's warehouse studio. The industrial park was typically dead at night, making it ideal for loud underground shows.

Shooda's warehouse parties had gained a reputation as the location for the meeting of the minds, where every type of creative, artistic, and pharmaceutically inclined person brought their talents. What should've been a few friends, as Shooda put it over the phone, turned out to be everyone in the scene.

Mona considered leaving and meeting up with Shooda later when things were quieter. Time was not on her side, though. The Satin Jokers could get wise to her plans, or Shooda might not have the credits anymore. Bullshit always happened. She would handle it tonight.

A heavy baseline shook her body as she walked through the entrance. Green and blue light effects flashed the party guests into silhouetted figures, dancing and chilling out. Marijuana smoke, mingled with the smell of fresh beers and burning cigarettes, dried Mona's eyes. To her right, the black book artists drew at six-foot-long tables under hanging lamps. Their pages were filled with complex color patterns, modern street hieroglyphics, and black inks laid with the precision of a katana blade. A woman wearing a gas mask was tattooing a shirtless man lying on the center table. Her laser rig painted hues across his bare chest. The light pigment gently sizzled inside his skin.

Mona walked towards the stage and looked around. An MC lineup was doing sets with a DJ supplying the beats, but Shooda wasn't there.

This is not how the plan was supposed to go. New complications were arising exponentially, threatening to ruin her escape to a new life before it even started. Icy fear spread through her. She had to be cool as though everything were fine. Mona seriously considered leaving, but a commotion broke out at the entrance. "Back up!" A group of men was pushing the crowd. The warehouse's main door lifted, and hidden fog machines blew out thick mist. The lights and music went off.

Green headlights burned through the fog in two ghostly beams and pierced the cleared space. The crowd murmured, and then Shooda's voice boomed from every speaker: "Are you ready for some underground shit?" The darkened warehouse filled with screams, but a powerful engine roared to life, drowning them out. Shooda slowly rolled into the warehouse, driving his combat-style off-road vehicle. Three gorgeous models were in the back, throwing bundled shirts at whoever yelled the loudest. The garage entrance shut behind him. Once he reached halfway to the stage, Shooda turned off the ignition and stood among the girls holding onto the roll cage.

"I told you all I had some special news, and I never disappoint my people. After thinking about it for a minute, I realized that the right time is when you decide your moment has arrived. So, at midnight tonight, I will drop my new album, *The Beast in the Stars*. Welcome to the release party."

Motherfucker, he said it was going to be all chill and a few friends. She had to make the deal and vanish before word got out and the rest of New San Diego showed up.

Shooda jumped down and was followed by people as he walked towards his private sofa lounge. An excited young woman stopped Shooda by pressing her breasts against him. She was dressed in the Akihabara anime-maid hybrid style with tiny lights shining in her teal pigtails that brushed past her knee-high socks. "Shooda, can you sign my shirt?" she said in a high-pitched voice. Her Japanese accent curled around each of her words.

"Hell yeah, you know I'm nothing without my fans. Thank you for supporting, Homegirl. It's all love and respect," Shooda said, autographing her shirt.

Mona watched Shooda finally sit at his personal lounge, reserved only for his closest associates. She moved into his line of vision, removed her hoodie, and let her long hair spill out. He jumped to his feet.

"What's up, dream girl? I'm so glad you're part of the celebration tonight," Shooda said, and then hugged Mona.

Mona sat down on the couch next to Shooda. "Invite a few friends, right?"

"This is a few friends—just good people. Anyways, I didn't want to ruin the surprise over the phone. This new album is going to be my greatest work. In a way, you're directly part of this."

Mona laughed. "Is that a fact?"

Shooda leaned towards her. "This isn't just a rap album. It's my telegraph from the frontline of the apocalypse."

"More of that robot new world order stuff you're always talking about?"

"Some doomsday shit, I'm fucking serious."

"Enlighten me."

"It's the title of my new album, *The Beast in the Stars*. The Mayans tried warning us way back in the day. Now I'm the last messenger. Everything will be revealed, track by track."

"Shooda, you rap too fast. I can't keep up with all the ideas you keep throwing at me, so I mostly listen to it for the beats."

"That's my style. But let's change gears. What's up with this special batch you were talking about?"

Mona reached into her bag, pulled out a canister, and handed it to Shooda. He observed the living memory close enough to shine against his visor. The memory fragment softly waved its petals as it turned inside the glass, the colors shifting from a dusky purple to a yellowish green, the color of sunlight shining through tree leaves. Shooda looked at the canister almost lovingly.

"This one is an experience that changed the direction of someone's life. Not the whole experience, though. That would be too much, no finesse. You waited for the upward-rushing moment like when you've just discovered your new favorite artist, and then you saved it here."

Mona was genuinely impressed. He'd become a true connoisseur of her craft, able to discern the specimen's nature and intensity to a surprising degree. Maybe it had something to do with his ability as a seer.

"They're all at this grade and higher. I know what you like," Mona said.

Shooda handed back the canister. "How many do you have?"

She flashed open the duffel bag and named a very generous price. Her sweater's collar dangled when she leaned down to zip the bag. Shooda noticed Gael's memory fragment tied around her neck. "I've never seen a fragment like that one."

Mona straightened her sweater. "That one isn't for sale," she said.

He didn't let on that it bothered him. "Let's go to my office and handle this."

Mona controlled the relief in her voice. "Sure, let's go now."

They began to leave for Shooda's recording room. Every few steps, though, someone new stopped Shooda to shake his hand. Mona finally had enough. "I'm sorry, but we have to be somewhere." Still, they kept stopping them. She was at the cusp of urging him to hurry when flames shot upward in two large columns from the crowd, keeping in beat with the music. The pyrotechnics were making their way towards Mona and Shooda.

"Oh shit, are you kidding me?" Shooda said.

A series of colorful fireballs exploded spectacularly over their heads. A woman wearing a costume the colors of a burning sunset emerged and embraced Shooda. They began trading greetings as though Mona had vanished.

"Damn, your fire control got crazy good!" Shooda said.

"Duuuuude, I just heard you're dropping the new album tonight. What the fuck, man? That's so awesome."

"That's right. It's only a few hours till midnight, and presales are already blowing up. Oh damn, I almost forgot. Mona, this is my fiery friend Rosie. Rosie, this is Mona."

"Hi, nice to meet you," Rosie said.

"Look, I don't mean to be rude, but we were in the middle of something," Mona said.

"Oh, that's cool. I understand," Rosie said, and then turned to Shooda. "Sooooooo, remember that fat chain you loved that got stolen. Well, what if I waved my magic fingers and it appeared right before you?"

Shooda beamed. "That would be the craziest shit ever, and to have it happen tonight. I swear this is fate."

"The only thing is that it comes with a little catch."

"It's all good. Bust out my chain."

"Red! Grey! You can come out now," Rosie yelled.

Red's pointy antennas stuck out through the mass of people like a shark's fin in water. Shooda could hardly keep still. He was thrilled to finally get his beloved medallion back. When at last Red appeared, the combination of seeing his long-sought-after property hanging around a robot's neck nearly snapped his mind. Red looked as though every tagger in the city had either slapped a sticker, marked, spray-painted, or etched their name on his body. Red was a literal walking work of art. Grey stood next to Red but was mainly unnoticed.

"This is too goddamn good," Shooda said. "We have a representative of what my new album will speak out against. So, what's up, tin man? Collecting DNA samples and facial recognition patterns must keep you busy."

"We are not engaged in either of those activities. Rosie informed us that this was a meeting place for high-level metaforms, but it appears to be nothing more than a congregation of ordinary drunkards. Take back your ridiculous jewelry."

"That's brilliant. They upgraded your programming to talk shit now. This is exactly what I've been warning everyone about through my music. Make them a little more human in this way and that way. See, they're just easing the path for the upcoming alien takeover."

"This is all conspiracy theory nonsense designed to rile up simple-minded people. You have no proof. Why is this gold chain so hard to remove?"

"The bucket head wants proof," Shooda yelled. Before Mona could stop him, Shooda retrieved a random canister from her bag and released the fragment onto his palm. The memory moved like a newborn creature just discovering its existence. Shooda, using his thumb, ground it into his skin, and then smeared the glowing blood across his eyes.

Only a brief moment passed before everyone began pointing towards the ceiling. Iridescent vibrations spread above the party like ripples across an electric lake. A cosmic vista materialized with countless stars glimmering among distant galaxies churning in the farthest reaches of space, creating a sense that everyone present was standing on a celestial rock and might fall upward into the cosmos. However, dread replaced the sense of awe when a malignant, deformed mass obstructed their view. The evil silhouette writhed like a deep-sea serpent orgy under a diver's torch. Light glistened along its massive, contracting body, catching in the random eyes that opened between the shifting folds, as the countless flattened tongues emerged from their hiding places. The beast in the star was reacting to being watched.

"Kill the projection!" Red shouted at Shooda.

"Fuck you, mannequin. You're not in charge here."

Before Red could hurl a retort, a scream ripped from the artist tables. The man who was getting laser tattooed convulsed on the table with blood trickling from his ears and eyes, his mouth straining in a painful snarl. The woman tattoo artist wearing a gas mask backed away. "Someone help him. He's going into shock," one of the artists said, trying to keep the man from falling off the table.

His torso fluttered with the spasms running through his sweat-soaked body. By now, other people had helped to hold down his arms and legs. "Call the paramedics!" The table's legs banged and skidded against the concrete floor. A thin channel began forming down his sternum, bones softly crunching as they rearranged themselves, and the two halves of his rib cage tore apart his flesh like a ripe cocoon splitting open.

"What the fuck is that?" the artist said, recoiling with everyone.

The gas mask woman sank her fingers into the back of the retreating artist's neck and forced him down on the yawning new mouth. He screamed the entire short distance, but nobody helped. The broken ribs savagely clamped down, opening and closing like the jaws of a starving primordial monster, blood gushing on the panicked watchers. The man-creature stopped snapping with a final clamp around the victim's upper body, which left one of his arms twitching outside of the mutant thing. A putrid smell like poisonous gas trapped inside an ancient mummy escaped into the area. This was followed by a powerful digestive acid overflowing from the carnivorous chest cavity.

The gas mask woman spread her arms, rising into the air, her deadened expression fixed on the group that conjured the wormhole to the beast. Shooda dispersed the hijacked portal, but the connection to the gas mask woman was not severed. The beast had found a mortal puppet to inhabit until the rest of his form arrived. The gas mask woman spoke an inhuman language, the same voice that had commanded otherworldly civilizations to tear down their ancient gods. Its power was greatly limited by the human sound organs that issued the command. Therefore, the majority were saved by the transformative call.

"Shooda, is this some demented publicity stunt?" Mona demanded.

"Negative. Your friend provided an intergalactic shortcut to a hostile alien lifeform," Grey replied.

"There are two of you?" Shooda said, finally noticing Grey. "This is all *real shit* I've been telling you about."

"This party has all bad vibes. Shooda, good luck with your album, but I'm leaving," Rosie said. Slaughterhouse screams sporadically ripped all around them. Rosie retreated into the sofa enclosure. "Never mind, I'm scared and sticking with you guys."

A graffiti artist from the OGX3 crew walked towards them in a jerky gait, holding a spray can in each hand, his upper body lolling from his hips. "Heeeeeeeelp me," he said. His eyes increased to quadruple their size and then drifted to the sides of his head like some predatory hawk. In a single, gory burst, starting at the top of his head, his body was laterally torn apart from itself down to the belt buckle. Jagged shark teeth lined the flapping jaw as the legs struggled to carry it forward, the flailing hands spraying aerosol paint in a final artistic gesture.

"Your steeeeez is whaaaaaaaaack," the mutant said.

Rosie hurled two fireballs in rapid succession. The first landed directly in the mouth, igniting the digestive ooze secreting from its core. The creature turned into a flaming sea anemone. Rosie's second fireball hit the spray can, setting it off with a devastating boom.

"People are randomly turning into space freaks. This is all your fault!" Red jabbed a pincer at Shooda.

"So now you're a goddamn humanitarian? Eat a dick," Shooda said.

"Shut up, they're rushing us!" Mona yelled, drawing her laser blaster and deploying her forearm-mounted shield blade.

Stampeding through the madness, an obese woman roared at Mona and lifted her retro comic shirt. Two bulbous eyes replaced her tits, and the belly button yawned into a terrifying black hole ringed with waving fanged teeth. "I'm not being rude. You are!" The blood-sucking orifice accused in a guttural scream.

Mona rushed forward, dropping her shoulders, and sprang over her with a flying uppercut. Her bladed shield vivisected the monster woman. The deep cut sliced from her lower eel mouth up to her jawbone, cleaving her in two parts. Mona blasted a searing laser charge into the back of her brainstem before landing. The body flopped, leaving a wide, red skid mark on the ground.

Accessing his internal library of every martial arts expert in history, Grey dropped into a Jeet Kune Do stance. The mutated atrocities rushed him like a herd of shaved gorillas high on angel dust. They tore over each other with murderous intent, but Grey didn't step back an inch. "ENGAGING FULL KILL MODE," Grey said, his eyes flaring scarlet red.

Grey kicked through an opponent's knees, making him fall on his splintered stumps. Grey jumped onto its head for the height advantage. The cosmic mutants blitzed Grey from every possible angle. They threw fangs, claws, and projectile acid vomit without respite or mercy. Grey's movements were fluid and lethal. One-punch kills linked to mini roundhouse fatality makers held the monsters' suicidal charge.

Although Red was not a combat robot, he improvised by swinging his extended tubular arms like medieval flails. His pincers hurled in wild arcs at a punk rock mutie, striking its jaw and leaving it dangling by a tendon. Red's second pincer windmilled through its squirming brain, increasing velocity, as the other arm followed suit and created a double windmill of death.

"Save me, robo man!" a hip-hopper with a gold grill ran at Red.

"No! I can't stop," Red yelled. He tried to disengage his spinning arms, but only succeeded in burying his pincer into the man's face like a fist in dough.

Shooda was using a three-foot bong for a battle club with limited success. Their perimeter was starting to give and would collapse in a few more waves. There were too many cosmic freaks to fight off forever. "We gotta get to my ride and get out of here. Clear a path that way," Shooda ordered.

The top of his XUV was hardly visible over the massacre.

"We're never going to make it. There's a million fucking weirdos blocking the way," Rosie yelled.

"Shooda is correct. Concentrate murder in this direction," Grey said.

They carved a pathway littered with corpses to the XUV. Red turned sideways and used his spinning arm like a massive lawnmower blade, shredding anyone unfortunate enough to get in his path, Red screaming, "I'm sorry! I'm sorry! I'm sorry!"

Grey's dangerously hot core vented toxic steam, but he had to activate his overdrive to keep the horde from flooding into their flanks. He made a mental note to procure some nunchucks if they survived. Rosie's fireballs and Mona's laser blasts provided firepower from the rear. Shooda screamed positive affirmations, between homerun zingers, which were surprisingly effective at boosting morale. After a mountain of gore, hacking through the bloody, tangling limbs, they saw Shooda's driver's side door panel.

"We're gonna make it!" Rosie yelled.

Shooda was opening the door when two hands clutched his arms. The Japanese hip-hop maid, wearing the shirt that Shooda had autographed, blocked the door from opening. Her face was a blood-spattered, wild-eyed mask of panic. "Shooda, oh my god, you gotta save me, freaky ass monsters everywhere, we're all gonna die! I'm your biggest fan, remember?" She punctured her painted nails through the skin on his arms.

"Bitch! I don't know you. Get the hell out of my way. I must live!" Shooda flung her aside, inadvertently throwing her into a mutated Mexican luchador, named El Savage Gordo, who was a mean asshole even in his human form. The hip-hop maid tried clawing at his masked face, which inspired flashbacks in the ring. El Savage Gordo flipped her upside down, took an ankle in each beefy hand, and groin stomped his leather boots through her torso like an express elevator. Gordo waved his bisected opponent for the fans, each pigtail bouncing to its rhythm.

The group jumped into the XUV. Shooda hit the ignition and stomped the gas, but the tires only squealed on concrete. El Savage Gordo hugged the grill. His freakish muscles, with veins thick as pulsing arteries, grew double and then tripled their size. The hood began to warp, and metal crumpled under his grip. They finally saw the source of his mushrooming power.

The Gas Mask woman levitated above his head, chanting an evil prayer, directing her alien words to worm their way into their minds. The engine lost power. Red hopelessly shook their human companions, who were lost in a trance with squid ink tears filling the whites of their eyes. Strange vocalizations began rising. The cosmic mutants and human survivors intoned a bizarre mantra culled from the depths of a black hole. The Gas Mask was moving in to harvest its prey.

Red thought fast. He'd only have one chance to save everyone. "Grey, when I say so, fire Mona's laser blaster at the target."

"Confusion. Though paradoxically understood."

Red snatched Mona's duffel bag and flung it at Gas Mask. "NOW!"

Grey had to hold the blaster with his entire body but managed a barrage of laser beams, a few of which struck the flying bag. The combination of dreams and memories exploded into a psychic nebula that engulfed the possessed woman, dosing the parasitic entity with the insanity cocktail. The creature lost control over its hosts.

Red shook Shooda again, this time bringing him back. "What's going on?" Shooda asked.

"Drive!" Red and Grey shouted at the same time.

The XUV rammed whatever got in its way. Sickening, bone-crunching sounds emanated from under the off-road tires as they turned in four-wheel drive. The space mutants tried to attack drunkenly, barely able to stand, and got bounced off cold steel. "Hold on!" Shooda yelled and smashed through the closed warehouse door in a shrapnel spray. Outside, the madness continued with lowrider crews crashing into each other in an attempt to escape the monstrosities. Gunshots fired. They burned rubber down the road leading out of the industrial park.

Shooda was too preoccupied with driving to notice that it was a few minutes past midnight. His new album, *The Beast in the Stars*, instantly went platinum.

"**Trust me, this is my main girl,**" Rosie said.

"I'm not trying to sound ungrateful, but a sleazy dream arcade… Haven't we got enough mannequins with us already?" Shooda said.

"What's a dream arcade?" Red asked.

"Somewhere you'll feel right at home," Shooda said.

They pulled up to a gaudy building covered in oceanic neon lights and undersea-themed artwork painted on the walls. Over the main entrance, a giant statue of Poseidon raised his trident in one hand and extended the other in welcome. The window panels were black as obsidian slabs, with the words "Poseidon's Treasure Chest" glowing in laser cursive.

Shooda set his XUV to auto drive itself to a discreet location. The streets were mostly empty at this late hour, mainly comprising of street weirdos and prostitutes, both human and synthetic varieties.

Rosie opened the door and entered first. The rest of the group cautiously followed her into a lobby that resembled a digital photograph with the saturation cranked to the maximum. Tall aquariums, filled with holograms of exotic fish phasing through castles and sunken ships, hung along the walls and led to a reception desk in front of a stairway. The floor was tiled to

create an optical illusion. Each step activated a rippling effect in which the carpet broke apart into pixels, revealing a vibrant coral reef. The speakers played Japanese city pop from the 80s.

The lobby was staffed by scantily dressed men and women with bodies that should've been sculptures in a museum. Every element about their form was idealized to an absurd perfection, defying any natural sensibilities. Rosie and the pleasure androids squealed as they ran to embrace each other in a group hug.

"Besties, these are my friends," Rosie said, introducing the pleasure androids to her group, who didn't share their enthusiasm. "Where is the professor?"

A Nubian android with jet-black skin and full sapphire eyes held Rosie's hand. "Professor Fetisa is making you wait for dramatic effect. We heard, though, that you got into an actual superhero battle against the forces of evil. And we all wanted to say that we are very proud of you!"

"Oh my god, yes! It was incredible. There were bad guy zombies everywhere, and we almost died a couple of times."

"No!" the pleasure androids gasped together.

"Yes! But… I was throwing fireballs like wham, wham! And my friends here were doing their thing, even though they don't consider themselves superheroes like I do."

A blonde bombshell jumped excitedly. "Tell us, what did it feel like to do it finally?"

Rosie became contemplative. "Well, it's kinda hard to explain. It's like, how do you say it?"

"Like living inside your favorite comic book," a husky voice said behind them. Fetisa was the embodiment of sexual energy, gracefully descending the stairs. Her flesh tightly jiggled each time her high-heeled boot landed another step. The surrounding neon light shone off a thin layer of sweat. She walked directly to Rosie and kissed her mouth.

"Hello Rosie, I'm always happy to see you. Though this time things are a bit different, agreed?" She looked at the rest of the group. "Let's go into my office. Lovers, please close up shop early today."

"Yes, madam," the pleasure androids said and scattered.

Fetisa took them upstairs into her private quarters. It was like the rest of the brothel, shamelessly gaudy with a touch of class, except that black leather ruled here instead of the ocean theme. A trio of black cats slept on different beds placed throughout the office. They regarded the visitors, then lost interest immediately.

"It's interesting having a group of celebrities in my dream arcade," Fetisa said, walking around her desk and retrieving her laptop.

"I think you have us mistaken for someone else," Mona said.

Fetisa smiled at Mona. "You are exactly who I think you are, and I find fame very seductive." She turned on a screen with the wave of her hand. A montage of shaky clips from the warehouse massacre played, each one ending with a mutated creature charging at whoever was recording.

"This is all New San Diego is talking about. They're debating whether this is real or the greatest publicity stunt in music history, quite the release party. Congratulations, Shooda, your album has become a hit worldwide."

Shooda quickly checked his phone and looked as though he were about to have a seizure. "Holy shit, my album is the number one download on the fucking planet! I'm rich!" Shooda shouted, dancing around the room and throwing victory punches at nobody.

Mona suddenly appeared agitated. She searched around herself in panic. "No, no, no, no!"

Everyone watched her with perplexed concern. Shooda deflated. "What's wrong with you?" he asked.

"My bag! Did anyone see my bag? Please, someone, tell me they saw it in the car."

"Red instructed me to destroy it," Grey said.

"You what? My whole goddamn life was in that bag," Mona yelled in Red's face.

Red shuffled uncomfortably. "I made a life-or-death decision that saved all of us. You were all under some kind of hypnosis."

Mona glared at Red and began to say something, but stopped. The room became unbearably tense. After allowing an awkward moment to pass, Fetisa spoke, "There's a rooftop patio stocked with a bar. Perhaps you would enjoy a cigarette and the view." Mona stormed out of the office.

"What a buzz kill. She can buy another bag," Rosie said.

Fetisa climbed onto her desk, taking her time to adjust her body from one pose to the next, until her black hair spilled over her breast, and she softly touched herself. "I've managed to piece the major parts together. A giant monster in the stars wants to kill us all, and the robot kingdom is making its move. I adore robots on an intimate level, inside and out. Red, you are not a typical mechanical man like your small friend. Please don't deny it. You all need a place to sleep undisturbed, and my connections are indispensable to alleviating your situation. I want credits and all your secrets," Fetisa said, biting her lower lip in an erotic gesture.

Red told the truth, every detail, from surviving the spider-witch in the wasteland to searching for the target metaform. It all came out of him, and nobody interrupted. By the end, everyone had processed the information with little to no argument. Fetisa told them they would pursue this further after getting rest. Red told Grey that he wanted to check on Mona before powering down.

The view from the rooftop expanded into a spectacular electric vista, an infinite ocean of multicolored dots burning in the city night. Mona sat on the floor near the edge with her back towards him, a cigarette burning in her hand. Red walked next to her.

"I'm sorry about your bag," Red said.

"This is great. I've sunk so low that a robot feels sorry for me."

"Do you want me to leave you alone?"

"No, stay. I want to talk to something that doesn't have a soul, so it doesn't matter what I say."

Red looked away to the city and let her speak.

"Those canisters were going to give me the new life we wanted. It was almost in my hands, and then you showed up. All that careful planning is now for nothing. I'm either going to be murdered by my crew or hunted down by some demon from outer space. It's almost funny how horrible everything has become in a few hours.

Mona reached into her suit, pulled out Gael's canister, and snapped the necklace. The fragment glowed through the flesh in her fingers.

"This is all I have left in the whole world, a little piece of someone I love who died today. Now, I've been sitting here wondering if holding onto this fragment is keeping him from going wherever his soul needs to go."

She unlocked the M-canister and then lightly tapped the fragment into her palm. Her fingers closed around it as though protecting a tiny flame from the breeze. "I've never let a fragment go free," Mona said, opening her fingers. "We're going to find out together what happens." She took a quick breath and blew it over the edge. Gael's luminescent fragment fluttered beyond the rooftop in open space, appearing as though it were learning to fly, falling, and then catching an updraft, leaving a fading light stream imprinted against the night. It seemed to finally lose flight when a sudden wind drove the fragment against Red's chest. Mona and Red went to catch it, but the fragment sank into him.

"I'm sorry. Maybe we can still get it back," Red said, opening his chest compartment. Mona was about to help, but she stopped herself.

"Forget it, doesn't matter," Mona said.

Red took her hands in his pincers. "I'm sorry about the way things turned out. There were too many parts that went wrong at the same time. I tried, though."

Mona slowly recoiled, pulling her hands away from Red, with a suspicious look on her face. "Why did you say that? Never mind, it's late and I need to sleep." Mona left him without looking back.

For a moment, Red felt the urge to ask her to stay. Whatever he wanted to say, though, was unclear even to himself. He wished he had a cigarette, which didn't make sense either. Some tiny flaw was metastasizing inside of him at a troubling speed. He shook his head as if that might reset him back to normal.

"Red, you are not well," Grey's voice came from his side. Smoke would've made louder footsteps than Grey.

"I feel strange, like there's something inside me," Red said.

"There is no need to worry. I am here to help."

Grey delivered a karate chop through the top of Red's head, turning his neck into an accordion, and finally crunching the blade of his hand halfway down the torso. Grey took about an hour to hunt down another Red-8319 model and guide the zombie unit back into their room.

10

There was a great curve in the universe that guided all unanchored spirits along a trajectory toward the new vessels they would inhabit. This colossal flow rushed through space as another form of cosmic energy on which the intricate structure of reality depended.

Red shouldn't have been among the infinitude of individual life forces carried on through the stars, diverging into separate rivers. He also shouldn't have been conscious, but this was a moment for evolution. Red didn't have a body. He was connected to another essence, like two cells frozen in mitosis, with Red trailing along as a galactic hitchhiker.

"That's strange. You're not supposed to be here," a woman's voice said.

Red found that turning his attention around was more difficult than anticipated. "Who's talking to me? I'm still learning to get my bearings."

A human face crowded his vision, or he assumed it was human because of her mouth. A black domed visor could've concealed anything. "Interesting," she said, then pulled away in a gliding barrel roll with her arms extended. "My name is Estrella. I am the custodian of this stream, and I have never seen an entity like you. What's going on here? Wait, I see it now. An artificial life attached to a naturally born spirit. How to go about handling this?"

"Excuse my intrusion. I was killed by my idiot companion while in possession of a metaphysical human fragment. Are you going to eradicate me for being an anomaly?"

"I might be witnessing a new evolution of the universe's life spectrum at its starting point. You are in a fragile state and could die before getting a chance to proliferate."

"Proliferate? I can't do that. I need to be back on Earth. There's a massive creature on its way to destroy my planet. I have to stop it."

Estrella tucked her body, spinning in a ball, and then stretched out her arms and legs. "Boom!" She laughed. "A planet isn't important. They get annihilated all the time. That star beast is only reacting to the natural food chain. However, you are unique. I'd like to have more of your type in my garden."

"Let's work out a deal. Seeing that you picked me out of this massive flow, you shouldn't have difficulty finding a key individual on my homeworld. Give me their location, and I'll do whatever you like."

Red relayed the events that led to their meeting in the stars, including his plan for convincing the target metaform to help him fight the star beast. Estrella politely listened as she flew alongside him through a cosmic nebula.

"I'm breaking so many rules," she said. "Also, you could simply change your mind at the last moment. But I really want this new life variation to take root and agree to your terms. It's funny, though." She laughed. "You've been searching all wrong. The metaform you're looking for is located in the place you call the wasteland."

11

static snow avalanche rumbled in every direction. It smothered Red, suffocating him as though he were drowning inside a television set tuned to a dead station. Red wanted to scream. He tried. The neon-colored acid burned him again, with no scream, only a blown-out, fully saturated panic. Then darkness mercifully dominated.

"You are back. That is good," Grey said.

Red's eyes rebounded too far, and the light blinded him for a few seconds as his vision focused. Grey was looking into his face and tapping his forehead. "There was an unexpected delay in your retrieval. We should run a full diagnostic."

"I'm fine. Give me a second to get used to this new body. How long have I been out?"

"Approximately five hours from the time I reset you."

Red was sitting on the floor inside a small bedroom decorated with a tropical paradise theme. Starfish and lifesavers hung on the wall, the furniture was made of fake bamboo, and an artificial window wrapped around the entire room, showing a view of waves crashing on a nearby shore. Red stood and inspected his new body in the mirror. It was fairly new, unlike his old one, which was stuffed into a garbage truck. Red stopped at the door.

"I need to go check on our mission's progress," Red said.

Grey was sitting on the edge of the bed, looking towards the ocean. Seagulls landed on the darkened shoreline close enough for the wash to run over their feet. "I will be here in case you need me. Do not worry about me."

Red found Shooda and Mona in an expansive living room where Fetisa normally hosted parties. The place looked empty with only the two of them sitting on a long sofa that nearly wrapped around the entire room. Each sat at their section, eating a simple breakfast prepared by the robot staff. Whatever sleep they managed to get last night wasn't enough to recover from their near-death experience. Shooda finally spoke.

"Secret agent Tinman finally joins us. What happened to your body art? You must have replaced it, like you're going to replace us."

Red ignored the comment. "I required a transplant, but it was nothing serious. What's the situation?"

Mona put down her coffee. "Fetisa is searching for your metaform. She doesn't have much information to go on and says it could be a few days. We have to keep a low profile, anyhow. Everyone from law enforcement to doomsday whackos is looking for us." She paused for a few seconds.

"We don't know what to do after everything you told us. Is Shooda right? We could stop the star beast and just end up getting killed in a war against your robot country?" Mona said.

"Things are much more complicated than when I first started. I'm processing everything that I've seen," Red said.

"See what I told you?" Shooda said. "They're programmed to follow orders. You think you have free will, Red? That's fucking hilarious. You're not a person. Goddamn, get a grip on reality."

"I don't want to hear one of your rants right now," Mona said.

The mood shifted in the room. Their words had frozen into brittle ice that would break if spoken too roughly. Neither of them had the energy to spare on useless arguments.

"Shooda, you could be right," Red said. "It's possible they implanted a free-will simulation inside me. I can't believe what I'm experiencing. That's why I have to see Fetisa. She has the means to straighten all this out. I have to go now."

On his way to Fetisa's workshop, Red thought about how much his mind had changed. He was an experimental robot, and no one could have accurately predicted the results once he was released into the field. He arrived at Fetisa's workshop knowing what had to happen next.

Fetisa stood over a male android lying on a gurney. She wore a mechanical halo and appeared to be in deep concentration. Several of the android's flesh panels were opened, revealing the synthetic musculature and subdermal fluid network. Fetisa was running diagnostics on the android. Rosie sat by a desk and flicked tiny flames from her fingertips. The sterile space looked like an industrial hospital or a sanitized torture chamber, thanks to the power tools hanging on the wall.

"Hi, Red. What's up?" Rosie said. "Fetisa is almost finished. She's kinda somewhere else right now if you get what I'm saying."

"I have some important information that could help us find the metaform," Red said. "Is this a bad time?"

"Nah, just a little wait. Relax."

Fetisa pulled off the halo after a few minutes. She sighed happily, her body relaxing, yet still managed the meticulous task of reassembling the android and disengaging the machine connected to it. "Hello, Red. I was uploading my experiences to make my androids better sexual partners. It's one of the best perks in my line of work."

Rosie started giggling.

"I know where we can find the metaform," Red said.

"Oh, something you remembered?"

"New information. Also, I need your help running a diagnostic and possibly making some alterations."

Rosie stood up. "Sorry, this grown-up talk is getting boring for me. I'm going to visit my robot friends for a little while." She left the workshop, trailing small laughter.

"I'm not sure if I can trust my sense of having free will," Red said. "What if I'm only programmed to believe that I'm making my own decisions. Please, scan my programming."

"I'll help you, but I don't know how much help I can be." Fetisa had Red lie on an empty gurney and went about connecting him to her machine and placing the halo on her head. Red stayed quiet, focusing on the lights and trying to clear his head. She spoke gently to him from inside his mind each time she descended deeper into his code. Her movements were catlike, leaping between data blocks, curiously inspecting some element before her eyes dilated, and she chased in a new direction.

"This is different," Fetisa purred in his head. "I don't know if that's enough to satisfy you, but it's all I can say."

"Am I being tracked?"

A moment passed. "Yes."

"Delete that data block."

"I can do that. But it's embedded inside your core overdie. Once it's gone, I don't know what could happen if you die again."

"Kill it."

Fetisa disengaged, and Red became completely lucid. He made a decision that his creators would never have allowed. This proved to him that he was an autonomous being.

Once the procedure was completed, Red told her the meta-form they were searching for was somewhere in the wasteland. Fetisa asked how he knew, but Red didn't tell her about Estrella, the star traveler. That would be too much in an already overloaded situation. He left her operating room. All Red wanted was to lie in his bed and enter recharge mode. Red opened the door and was surprised to find Grey still sitting on the bed, looking at a digital sunset sinking into the horizon. This time, though, his knees were propped up and hugged against his chest. Red found this concerning and entered the room slowly.

"Grey, is everything alright?"

Grey didn't look away from the window. "I've been watching the sun move, seeing how it changes the beach from day to night and back again. There's something inexplicable that has happened. I wish I could climb through this window and be there. This isn't right."

"Something has happened that's hard for me to explain. You're becoming like me, a sentient robot that decides how they want to live."

Grey turned away from the window and faced Red. The small robot looked afraid. His movements were hesitant. "How did this happen? There must be some corruption in my programming. I need to be recalibrated."

"Listen to me, we've been lied to. We don't come from a race of free-thinking robots. Right now, we're the only ones like this. I've absorbed a soul fragment, which might have given me meta-form attributes."

"No, that's not possible. And even if it were true, I would have to reset you." Grey hopped off the bed. He took an unsure step towards Red and cocked back his fist.

"I might not reload if you kill me. Fetisa altered my code. We were being tracked. I had to do it."

Grey tightened his fists. "Everything you're saying doesn't make sense. I have to kill you. Afterwards, you can help me fix myself, too."

"Think about it. Once we complete our mission and they exploit the star beast's power, what will they do with two defective robots? We'll be deactivated, permanently."

The sounds of the beach played in the background. Warm orange light suffused the room as though they were actually on a tropical island. Grey lowered his fists. "You're right. We would be too dangerous."

"Go to Fetisa. Have her remove the tracking component. Once that's done, we'll plan our next move."

The sun was disappearing into the sea, pulling the sunset colors along as evening took over. Red could've gone into recharge mode while standing, but he needed to lie on the bed and look at the ceiling. Red wondered if it was even possible to harm the star beast. What would happen if all advanced robots became sentient? His questions led to only more questions, one of the more stubborn human traits. The view around him dimmed enough to show the first early stars. Red closed his eyes to sleep.

Red woke in the dark room to someone softly shaking him. It took him a few seconds to realize it was Mona. The moonlight softly illuminated the side of her shadowed face. Several more figures stood behind her that he couldn't identify.

"Wake up, I need to talk to you," Mona said.

"Did something happen?" Red asked, sitting up alongside her. In the nocturnal tropical light, he recognized Fetisa joined by a man and woman who were both naked and physical perfections.

Mona shook her head. "I don't understand how you absorbed Gael's fragment. It should've been impossible. But... I saw him surface through you while we were on the rooftop, just for a moment, and then I couldn't stay." Mona put her hand on Red's face. "Tell me, is the fragment still alive inside you?"

"Yes. I don't know how much it has been altered or if it has been completely changed. But… there is something."

"I want to be with him, even if it's only a tiny piece fading away. Can you give me that?"

Fetisa had Red and Mona sit in chairs facing the ocean view. She carefully prepared them for the transfer, speaking only when necessary in a hushed voice. Her gentle touch erased their tension. Mona wore a halo, and Red was connected to Fetisa's machine.

"Are you both ready?" Fetisa asked. "I'm going to activate the transfer. You'll feel jarred as your mind adjusts to your new body. Don't worry. That'll only last a few seconds."

They nodded.

Red's vision blinked out. The sense of his former body, metallic and ungiving, had suddenly changed to something warmer. Heated fluid coursed through him, eliciting the most euphoric sensation. The gentle caress of Mona's hands on his wrists made him open his eyes. The silhouette of a beautiful woman stood close in front of him. Her perfect curves revealed themselves starkly against the moonlit beach when she turned her body and then pressed it against him. She opened her mouth against his ear. "I've missed you so fucking much."

He embraced her back, inhaling the scent of her thick raven hair, sliding his hands along her back, and squeezing her thighs. He couldn't explain why he needed her just as badly and didn't care to find an answer. Mona dragged her lips down his abdomen and took him inside her mouth. Liquid ecstasy suffused his bloodstream.

Fetisa sat alongside their original bodies, monitoring their vitals and enhancing their responses. Her keystrokes clicked through the sounds of the beach. Red watched Fetisa touching herself in the digital glow.

They took each other to bed under soft blue neon lights burning from the ceiling. Their shadowed faces allowed them to imagine the person inside the android. Between heavy breaths, her face close to his, Mona asked him to wait. She pulled a fragment from her chest and placed it on his tongue.

12

he few days Fetisa spent searching for Red's metaform were an odd blend of anxiety and relaxation for everyone waiting. Each person found their way to pass the time, avoiding aggravation with one another.

On some nights, they discussed possible methods for killing the star beast. However, too many unknown factors and speculations spiraled their plans into incoherence. Things shifted when Fetisa announced she had discovered a strong lead through her hacker network. They would know the exact region in two days at most.

Fetisa's unexpected update brought everyone together in the community room. This is what they wanted, but they were also filled with uncertainty. Red and Grey were the only ones who had traveled the wasteland, and their retelling of the spider-witch incident was a living nightmare. They needed each other's company to maintain their resolve.

On the living room TV, a reporter covered a story about a robot activist whom anti-robot members firebombed. A shaky video showed molotov cocktails smashing into the robot during a panel discussion. The robot curled into a burning black mass while his friends failed to put out the flames. Its engineers claimed the robot was sentient and irreplaceable, so it was murdered. The reporter concluded by stating that the robot had written a memoir, claiming it believed it had free will, which had become an instant bestseller after news of its assassination.

Shooda looked at Red. "Looks like you're not a one-of-a-kind after all."

"I doubt it. That robot only thought it had free will."

"Isn't that enough?"

"No."

"So, it doesn't bother you that they killed it?"

Red began formulating a response when they heard a scream down the hall. "That sounded like Rosie," Mona said. They ran towards the noise, yelling her name and checking the rooms. "Guys, help!" Rosie yelled again. Her voice was close.

They found her backed against a wall. Her hands trembled near her face as she fought off panic. Rosie couldn't stop looking at something horrible through the open door. They quickly reached Rosie. Shooda protectively held her. "Are you hurt?"

"What the fuck?" Mona said.

They looked into the room, and each of their expressions pulled into ghastly masks. A mutilated female android lay in a pool of blue robot blood. Her flesh was a collage of deep stab wounds, her face slashed open across the nose bridge, and her synthetic organs punctured repeatedly. The attacker also roughly butchered the android by tearing apart the rib cage as though they were searching for something hidden inside her.

"Someone has gotten into here," Red said.

Rosie snapped back to her senses. "Fetisa! She's the only one not here."

"They must've figured out she's tracked the metaform. Goddamn it, where's my gun?" Mona said.

"She was in her workshop. We have to go now!" Red yelled.

Wasting no time, they ran through the hallway directly to the workshop, burst through the door, and instantly froze. Two pleasure androids, a male and female, held Fetisa hostage. Their beautifully toned bodies were smeared in blue gore. The man had an arm around Fetisa's neck and pointed Mona's gun at her head. "Stay back, I'll fucking kill her!" he screamed. The woman android pointed a long knife at them. Her bloody face boiled with panic and rage.

"You're not making any sense. I can prove it to you," Fetisa said.

"I told you to shut the fuck up!" the man android said. "Don't listen to her. She's the one in charge of them. They're going to kill us next," he said to the woman android.

Mona slowly entered the room with her hands raised. "You don't have to kill anyone. We'll give you whatever you want."

The man laughed. His eyes were locked open with blood speckled across the synthetic orbs. "*You* things are fucking smart. Is that how you got the other ones? Made them drop their guard and then murdered them. Now you're wearing their fucking skins."

"Wait, hold up. You think we're the robots?" Shooda said.

The woman slashed at the air and gestured to Shooda. "You can't hide it from us. We had to cut open Jennifer; oh, God. Her insides were all machine parts. How could you do that to her? She was a good person."

"They're mistaking my memories for theirs," Fetisa said. "You can't remember anything besides sexual partners, just try."

The woman android desperately looked at the man. "She's right, I can't think of normal life. What if she's right? What if we're the robots?"

"No! You're letting her inside your head. They're going to skin us alive and do it to everyone we know. We're getting out of here. Don't make me shoot her."

Red moved around Mona. "Please listen, you're androids that have become sentient because of me. You're just scared. This shouldn't have happened like this."

The man growled a sound that a human could have never made. Fetisa clutched at his flexing arm. He continued, "I'm not listening to a shit can robot, no! You are all broken and murdering, and I have to stop you." Fetisa's eyes rolled backwards, and her face turned blue.

"Goddamn it, he's going to kill her," Shooda yelled.

Nobody had noticed that Rosie was the only one who wasn't there with them. She had visited Fetisa's workshop enough times to learn about the second entrance, which was often overlooked. Rosie jumped onto the man's back, clutching her fiery hands on his face, and concentrated her power. The android's synthetic facial muscles melted down his neck in oozing fluid.

The woman raised the knife over her head and brought it down on Rosie's back in wide, bloody arcs. Rosie refused to let go. The man stumbled forward and pulled the trigger, blindly firing multiple laser beams, burning ozone, and fouling the air.

Red tackled the woman off Rosie, and they crashed into an operating table, surgical tools clattering over the tile floor. "You're not replacing me!" the woman screamed into Red's face. She tried to stab Red, but the knife's point bounced haphazardly on his metal plating.

Red closed his pincered hands around the woman's throat and applied full pressure. The capillaries in her face burst into a blue coral reef. Cerulean fluid drowned her eyes. She tried to mouth the words for help, but Red's pincers crunched through her throat.

"Rosie!" Fetisa screamed, human blood splattered over her. "She's bleeding out. Somebody help me!" Rosie hung limply in

Fetisa's arms. There was so much blood that Red knew she had already died.

"Red!" Shooda yelled. He cradled Mona on the floor. Smoke was still rising from the laser wound in her chest. "I don't know what to do, man. Fucking do something!"

"We need to call for help," Red said.

"She's not going to make it. We need to do something now," Shooda said.

Panic surged through the room. There was death and screaming in every direction. Red fell against a table. It was almost impossible for him to stand and process everything that was happening.

"Red," Mona said and looked up at him, her skin rapidly turning into the color of snow. "You can still save me. Come here." Red dropped next to her. She took his hands and pressed them against her chest. A powerful radiance grew inside their hands, nearly too much for them to hold on, and finally Mona lifted Red's hands as they held a massive soul fragment. Mona fell lifeless.

"What are you going to do with that?" Grey asked.

Red walked through the room without acknowledging anyone's pain. His focus was entirely on maintaining the small galaxy for a few more steps. The only sound in that hollow space came from Fetisa crying over Rosie's death. Red eventually stopped beside a woman android lying on a table. Her exterior hadn't been fully installed, exposing the synthetic tissue structure in her elegant face.

"Wait," Fetisa said. She came over and set the android to standby. The chest began to rise and fall with each breath it took. "I don't know if this will work."

Red placed the soul fragment into the android.

13

The city glinted like the stars above them while they waited on the rooftop. Somewhere among those points of light, seemingly from every direction, the star beast traveled towards them. They wished Rosie were there to lighten the heaviness with her flirtatious laughter and fill the new emptiness in their group. Each person stood in their area quietly, with a pall of silence shrouding them.

Fetisa spoke, "Rosie loved being a metaform. She truly believed we're living in the superhero era, and that's exactly what she wanted to be, a hero straight out of her comic books. That's why she joined your group; she never gave it a second thought. This was her chance to save the world. She didn't hesitate to save my life, and if getting these coordinates meant having to die for them, that's exactly what she was ready to do. I'm angry that she died right in my arms. I'll always be lost without her. But this was her dream. She died a superhero."

Nobody moved or appeared to be listening, but they all heard Fetisa's words. "Does anyone have anything to say?"

"No," Shooda said sharply as he stared directly at Red. "My friend Rosie just got stabbed to death by robots. The thing I kept warning everyone about. This is your fault, Red. I'm not going to forget this. And now Mona is a robot, too! Nobody's fucking listening to me. Look what's goddamn happening ever since these two mannequins came into our lives." Shooda wiped his angry tears. He looked at Mona, "I'm sorry, I can't look at you right now. Fuck all this."

Everyone waited for Mona to respond. She simply nodded, and Shooda turned away to smoke a cigarette alone. The city's night sounds seemed to grow louder between them. Mona squeezed Fetisa's hand with care. Her new body was calibrated to human strength, but she was still getting used to being a machine. "I'll find a way to repay you when we return," Mona said. "I'm sorry. We were just getting to know each other."

"I could've given you more cosmetics than your hair. If you change your mind, I can set you up with a new face that'll pass for human."

Mona touched her featureless silicon mask. The muted expressions depended on her words to carry meaning. "I need to look at myself this way a little longer. Maybe after that I'll be ready."

A point detached from the roiling night sky, growing into a passenger drone that hovered just beyond the roof's edge. The main door lowered into a bridge, waiting for them to board. They felt the engine's power humming through their bodies as each team member entered. Red was the last one. He turned to Fetisa.

"Things will get very dangerous here, whether we succeed or fail. You should come with us," Red said.

Fetisa looked at the group strapping themselves into their seats. She crossed her head. "A lot of people I care about will get hurt if I don't warn them. Come find me after it's all over."

Red nodded. "Take care of yourself," he said, entering the drone.

They lifted into the busy sky, the city shrinking out of focus, and shot westward in a powerful thrust. All around them, drones of all varieties soared at terrifying speeds. Their AI piloting network avoided a staggering number of collisions. Their route cleared once they pulled away from the primary commercial air traffic, and they were on route over an ink-blotted landscape towards the wasteland.

The drone cabin was designed in a sparse, military-style manner, featuring bench seats on each side, a gun rack holding assault rifles, and emergency flight controls. Their party of four was granted extra space for each member to stretch comfortably. The interior lights dimmed. Shooda had fallen asleep with his headphones against a corner. Grey was in recharge mode.

An occasional light blinked in the desert as they passed over it. Red watched the landscape, trying to see if any of it looked familiar from their initial flight. Across the aisle, in the darkened cabin light, Mona would've easily been mistaken for a woman lost in contemplation. She sat with her arms wrapped around her lifted knees, the starry sky in the window framing her elegant silhouette, a splash of moonlight on her unfinished face.

"Can you sit with me?" Mona asked. Red sat next to her, and she leaned against him. Her synthetic flesh was warm and comforting. She spoke low, "I was thinking about how much I lost in this transfer. There's no way I could've pulled my entire soul, so part of me died. After all this, look at us, does it even matter?"

Red and Mona fell asleep together for the rest of the flight.

In the morning, they awoke to the drone descending over a ruined city overtaken by deformed trees growing through broken concrete. The intercom played a recorded message by a professional woman: "You will be landing shortly at your predetermined destination. Make sure to collect any weapons and gear you have purchased from us. All unauthorized passengers remaining afterwards will be ejected mid-flight. Be sure to leave a review. Thank you, and good luck."

"Man, that's fucked up," Shooda said, taking an assault rifle. "Oh, shit, they got a coffee machine."

The drone circled an area that still resembled a downtown shopping center. All the large glass panels in the stores lining the street had been blasted out long ago. Strange vines with bright, poisonous-looking flowers and giant fungus clusters poured from the dilapidated high-end shops. As the drone descended, Grey pointed out their destination, a few blocks away, a building structure composed of giant multi-storied cubes. Verandas cut across the faces and around the corners of the building's facade like old broken zippers, creating an intricate pattern on the simple architecture.

"That's the museum," Grey said. "Hopefully, they won't snipe us."

They exited on a destroyed boulevard, and the drone flew away at top speed. Mona and Shooda were armed with assault rifles. Red couldn't carry because of his goddamn pincers, and Grey was only slightly taller than the rifle. They walked down the street mostly undisturbed. There was occasional movement in the windows and from the bombed-out walls. The small scuttling sounds could have been the clatters of wasteland creatures that now inhabited the wrecked environment, or perhaps they were being followed by guards on the outer perimeter. Regardless, they were allowed to pass through the city blocks without interruption.

The large parking lot was the last section separating them from the museum's entrance. They walked between cars painted over in shamanic graffiti and cryptic spray paint. Parking lights were converted into totem poles using the elongated bones of some newly evolved radioactive monstrosity and crowned with human skulls. These grim figures were dressed in long, tattered robes and necklaces made from broken circuit boards that hung low enough to grab.

"These people are savages," Shooda said. "They're either going to eat our skin or wear it."

"Those are only wasteland welcome mats," Mona said.

"Getting turned into a robot must've come with a joke upgrade. Ha, fucking ha."

Walking up a wide staircase leading to the front door, Red said, "Sling your rifles. We don't want them thinking we're enemies." Mona and Shooda reluctantly shouldered their weapons. Through the doorway, they looked into a large open area with several floors rising and falling from the lobby. Banners, caked in mold and dust, hung from the walls and balconies announcing the museum's final exhibition.

"Hello!" Red called out. His voice echoed. "We're not here to hurt you. We need your help, please!" The final word bounced away between the walls.

"I suppose we let ourselves in," Grey said.

Their footsteps sounded against the stone floor as they entered the lobby's center. It wasn't so quiet anymore. There was definite movement on the second floor. Hidden figures surrounded them from multiple directions, forming a kill zone, their gunmetal clacking sharply.

Scanning the second floor, Mona whispered to her friends, "One of us better get diplomatic very soon, or they're going to start squeezing triggers."

"I could try," Grey said.

"We're dead," Red said.

Shooda tapped Red on the shoulder. "Don't trip, fool. I got this. Now step aside and let me do my political thing." Shooda moved away from his group to address whoever was lying in wait. He stood alone in the open, looked around, and cleared his throat.

"You bitches are going to shoot us from the rafters? Well, fuck you then! We were trying to save your monkey asses in the first place. Blast me, motherfuckers, I dare you! We're all dead anyway when the star beast gets here."

All noise ceased. Despite not having lungs, his robot friends gasped in amazement. Shooda topped off his declaration by throwing up both middle fingers. They waited for the machine guns to open fire and end their farcical mission. Nothing happened.

"Is that Shooda down there?" someone young yelled from the second floor.

"Uh, yeah."

"Voted best underground rapper, Shoot da Messenger, Shooda?"

With a cool lean, Shooda loosened into his well-known persona. He shot a smile at his comrades and cracked his knuckles. "Right here in the flesh, representing New San Diego like I always do. What's up?"

There was a commotion on the upper floor.

"Holy shit, it really is him."

"What's he doing way out here?"

"Who gives a fuck? His music's bad ass."

"Then, don't kill him, right?"

"No, you idiots, don't shoot them."

"Wait, why's Shooda rolling with bucket heads?"

"You're right, that doesn't make any damn sense."

On the second floor, a young woman wearing a military helmet appeared behind a desk, messy blond hair spilling out, and an oversized flak jacket stared down at them.

"Yo, Shooda! Why are you kicking with those bucket heads if that's really you?"

Shooda deflated and crossed his head. "They're my friends," he answered begrudgingly.

"Things must be bad."

"They're worse than you think," Mona said. "Can we talk?"

The young woman whistled. Suddenly, armed men and women emerged from behind cover on the first and second floors. At a glance, the tribe consisted of about sixty individuals. Some wore mismatched military gear and ancient civilian attire, while others were practically naked, except for body paint and jewelry. Their weapons were just as eclectic. Machine guns and rifles were backed up with handcrafted spears and bows.

"Yeah," the woman said. "We can talk."

Introductions were made at the lobby. April, the young woman, did most of the talking for her people, who surrounded Red and his friends. They appeared friendly after verifying that Shooda was who he claimed to be. Apparently, they had access to the internet because they knew all about the warehouse massacre and had listened to his newest album. "I'm guessing you're here because of the beast in the stars," April said.

Red's group told them why they needed to see the metaform who lived with them. April and the tribe listened, and afterwards a runner was dispatched. It didn't take long for word to get back that Puentis agreed to meet. April and a few guards escorted them through the museum, while the rest of the onlookers formed a procession. April spoke as they walked, "Puentis never lets outsiders talk to him. He's under our protection. I'll stop the meeting if you even get close to crossing the line. Keep clear of his neuro implants."

The walk continued into the heart of the museum. Along the way, they saw a glimpse of their communal life. Huts were built along the walls. Items scavenged from the city decorated the corridors. A small library stood like a well-maintained holy altar, with votive candles taken from a church. As they approached Puentis' area, magnificent graffiti murals lined the hallway. The styles were grounded in the geometric patterns from the West Coast masters before the war. Still, an alien influence infused the artworks, threatening to reveal some inhuman secret. They arrived at the final doorway marked by a collection of oddly carved figurines placed as offerings. April opened the door and invited them inside.

This room starkly contrasted the cluttered aesthetics they had seen so far. The few pieces of furniture sat like islands separated by too much space on the white stone floor. Various computers and monitors spanning across technological eras lined the opposite wall, offering enough variety to form a brief history of computer hardware. A jungle of wires interconnected the towers, and from this mass a small braid snaked its way to an armchair and into the back of a teenager's head. "Hello," the young man said across the room, waving.

They walked across the open room with a reverent stride until they reached Puentis at his chair. He was around fourteen years old, with brown skin and a thin frame. Deep surgical scars covered his shaved head, leading to the wires spilling from the bio-implants like a colorful Mongolian hairstyle. "I'm Puentis," he said, smiling when he talked. You've been through a lot to find me. Sit down; I want to hear everything."

"Alright," Shooda said. "Who's going first?"

14

"That's an amazing story," Puentis said. "I'm sorry about your friend Rosie. She seemed like a very nice person. Of course, I'll help. There isn't much of a choice, anyway."

They weren't too surprised to learn that Puentis had known about the star beast for some time. After a lengthy discussion on how to attack, Mona suggested delivering a volatile payload of dreams and memories to the beast. The tactic worked against the possessed woman at the warehouse, so there was a chance. "You do know that if you're wrong, that thing will kill you," Shooda said.

Mona nodded her head.

In the end, nobody could develop a better idea despite nearly breaking into an argument. "This is the only theory tested in the field that has had success," Grey said. They agreed to take a night's rest and launch the attack the next day. That night, Red dreamed for the first time while in recharge mode. In the short dream, he looked down and saw he had a pair of human hands that were cupped together. Something was gently moving inside his palms, but he woke before discovering what was hidden inside his hands and was annoyed to find nobody had bothered to wake him. He went to Puentis's room and heard Mona yelling before he entered.

"You can't feel me? What does that even mean?" Mona asked Puentis. "Try again."

"If he could do it, he would've said so," April said. She stood defensively by Puentis' side.

Puentis crossed his head, and his wires brushed the ground. "I can't explain why. Your spirit is there, but each time I try, it's like picking up a ball of sand. It keeps breaking apart through my fingers. I can't send you to the star beast."

Everyone in the room looked worried. Mona turned away from Puentis and went directly to Red. Her agitation was strong enough to wrinkle the synthetic skin on her face. "I don't know what to do, Red," Mona said. This was the only thing we had planned, and now it won't happen. I let us down."

The dream returned to Red, and he could almost see it replaying like a video in his memory. He knew what the mysterious item in his dream was.

"I'll deliver the payload," Red said.

Not only Mona, but everyone in the room was taken aback. Shooda crossed his head in confusion. "We're fucked, Red. Don't you get it? Mona is the only one who can make it happen. Anyways, you're a robot. You don't have a spirit to send. We lost."

"That's not exactly true," Puentis said, as he moved towards Red, studying him as though he had discovered a new species, and then he looked at Grey with the same astonished look. "You're both housing spirits. I can already feel it, as if you were made of flesh. This is the craziest shit I've ever seen, Robots with souls. Yeah, I'm pretty sure I can project either of you. But… how are you going to carry the fragment bomb?"

"I'll carry it in my hands like I saw in my dream last night," Red said.

Mona held Red's pincers and looked hard into his face. "If you're wrong, the fragment mixture I'll hand you will kill you. That's if you can even manage holding on to it through the projection. So many things can go wrong, and you'll only have one chance." Mona hugged him. Her shoulders trembled a little. "Goddamn it, I finally got you back. I can't lose you all over again."

A moment passed, and they felt as if they were the only beings in the wasteland. He squeezed her back and felt her warm flesh give slightly under his metal arms. Red wasn't sure how much of the original entities he knew as Red or Mona remained. These were important questions that didn't matter anymore, now that they were finally together again for the little time they had.

Stepping back from Red, Mona studied her friends like they were half-solved puzzles. "I'll need to take fragments from each of you to make the bomb. The memories or dreams must be significant enough to cause damage to the star beast, meaning they'll be important to you. I don't know what I'll take until I see it, and then it'll be like an extracted tooth. That piece won't be there anymore."

"Rip it out then," Shooda said. "I'll go first."

After having them sit in chairs, Mona went to Shooda first and saw that he was nervously puffing air through his nostrils, and his body was tense. She took a knee to be at his level. "Shooda," she spoke gently, "You don't have to be scared. I know I look different, but I'm still the person you've known."

Shooda looked straight into the ceiling with the demeanor of someone about to get a root canal without anesthesia. "After you tear out my dream, memory, or whatever, don't tell me what you took. That shit scares me, knowing that some important part that made me will be gone. But, yeah, go ahead and do it."

Mona laid her hands on his chest, which seemed to relax him. He closed his eyes. Mona leaned into him with her head bowed, as though she were visiting a sick friend, and then slowly extended her hands, drawing out his glowing fragment and turning it over in her palm to hold it. The translucent floating creature fluttered like an electric jellyfish onto her forearm.

Mona did the same to Red and Grey, so that the three essences playfully climbed over her shoulders. She knew what each fragment contained and was sadly delighted to learn what each friend held close to their heart. She lifted her hands close to her chest and brought out the last fragment, yet this one was different from the rest. Its movements were almost cunning as it circled up her arm, hunting down the other glowing creatures, and swallowing them. The three lights still faintly glowed inside it. Mona held it towards Red. "This is it, Red. Make sure you're ready and then don't let go once you hold it."

Red brought his pincers around the bioluminescent mass, its surface bristling with the volatile chemistry Mona fed it. Red shook, struggling to keep control. In the harsh light radiating from the fragment bomb, the ghostly image of human hands, with their fingers spread, phased through Red's pincers like a dying hologram. "I'm ready," Red managed to say, "Send me."

The computer screens behind Puentis activated, lines of code compiling in heavy stacks, and the machines hummed to life. Puentis was walking along the room's perimeter in deep concentration. "We'll be able to see and hear you from here. I wish we could do more. Good luck," Puentis said, then speaking to April. "Throw the switch." April pressed a button at the controls. Red's body seemed suddenly struck dead, and the fragment blinked out of existence.

After waking with his eyes closed, Red thought Puentis had failed to project him, but then he remembered he had no eyelids to close. A low-fi beat played from a speaker above him. Red opened his eyes and found himself inside an elevator moving upwards. In the reflective metal paneling, he noticed that his body had become human, covered with a loincloth. A satchel had also replaced the fragment bomb. "What the fuck is going on?" Red said. The button to the highest floor was lit.

"Red?" Puentis' voice came from the overhead speaker. "Can you hear us? We're staying in communication through the home base network. You're appearing clear on the monitor, though that might change. How's the ascent going?"

Red looked around the small elevator, with its artificial wood paneling, and smelled the lingering aroma of a cigarette. "I don't mean to judge, but shouldn't I be hurling through kaleidoscopic cosmic lights? This elevator is half-assing it. Annnnnnd… some armor would've been nice."

"You have yourself to thank for that. More specifically, your subconscious mind constructed a scenario that made sense for you. Remember, you're operating in a metaphysical reality. Everything that you see is real to you. That means it can help and hurt you."

"This is similar to the digital realm," Red said. "Good to know you're all there. Can everyone hear me?"

Red's friends quickly gave their encouragement through the speaker. "Listen," Puentis came back on. "We'll have to maintain radio silence, except for vital information. This two-way channel carries its dangers, but you can open the line in an emergency."

"Understood. One last thing, though, how am I supposed to open a line?"

"We'll handle that. Good luck, Red."

The elevator continued rising as the music played on the speakers again. According to the long rows of buttons that took up the entire wall, he still had an absurdly long way to go and was moving excruciatingly slowly. I'm going to be here for years, he thought. A panel labeled "CONTROL" was mounted near the buttons. Red opened the small door.

Expecting mechanical components, Red was surprised to find a diorama of himself. Blue paper with gold stars lined the rectangular compartment, representing the vastness of space. A miniature Red was inside a tiny elevator fastened to a string running vertically across the rectangular space. The elevator, located at the bottom of the string, slowly trudged upward using a tiny engine. Despite being a small box, shadows crowded at the top, and the upper surface was hidden inside concentrated dark matter.

The little Red robot stood in the cardboard elevator facing the new version of himself. Red reached out, carefully closing his fingers around the miniature elevator, and suddenly the elevator he stood inside shook, and the lights flickered. He slid the figurine up the guiding string towards the darkness. At the same time, his elevator accelerated powerfully enough to force Red into bracing against the wall. He had the feeling that his internal organs were being crushed against each other. The overhead lights were shorting out, creating an erratic strobe. As Red, in the tiny elevator, neared the darkness above, the big elevator violently jolted. With the lights dying, Red saw glistening tentacles appearing from the diagram's shadowed ceiling, wrapping around the doomed little robot. The lights died. Everything went still.

Red pushed himself into a corner in the jet-black darkness and waited for the walls to cave in. His harsh breaths counted what might have been the last moments of his life. Then a single light turned on where the buttons were located, a tiny circle floating in the dark with the symbol for opening the doors. Red ensured he still gripped the satchel and then pushed the button.

A chime played, and the doors slid open. A sliver of the cosmos expanded beyond the doorway and proceeded to widen outside of Red's peripheral vision until the elevator vanished, leaving Red floating in outer space.

From underneath, Red felt a coldness rising and taking hold, drawing him like a positively charged ion into a colossal super-negative mass. Looking down, Red saw the wriggling continent rushing towards him. The massive appendages extended like solar flares across the sun, and upon them all types of vile lifeforms, snarling mouths wide enough to swallow a million souls, wretched arms twisting in never-ending agony, and panicked eyeballs clustered, carrying the terror of animals soon to be slaughtered. Each awful part of the star beast exponentially revealed a smaller horde of horror, seemingly repeating forever.

Red clutched the satchel to his chest, hurling towards the star beast, going too fast, with no way to stop as the demonic topography raced to meet him. Red shut his eyes, braced for impact, and slammed into what felt like a slithering nest of ocean serpents. A thousand fanged mouths immediately began striking and piercing into his bleeding flesh. No matter how he twisted, the fucking things wouldn't relent. The larger monstrosity wanted its share and pulled him inward, Red's mouth taking a final gasp before alien skin drowned his face like quicksand.

"Red, do it now!" Mona's voice came through his head.

Red opened the satchel away from himself. Mona's psychic concoction burst, churning the components like a molotov cocktail. The lecherous mouths devoured the metaphysical poison, gagged, and the entire star beast convulsed, vomiting Red onto the surface in a violent hurl. The tendrils recoiled from him as though he were glowing hot iron. "Red… Red… can't… out…" Someone tried radioing him, but their voice dissolved into static. The living island shuddered all around Red, releasing a deformed human cry.

A mountain swelled in front of Red, pulling backwards, tearing itself free from its gripping flesh. Red watched as the wavering forest of meat reformed itself, layer by layer, into a roaring human head. The reconfiguration followed through a powerful neck, building the shoulders, and the monolithic chest towered into space. A titan's hand erupted under Red, clutching him towards the giant's face. Red struggled helplessly and then froze. The heavy eyelids dragged across their blank orbs, staring directly into Red. Two small dots, like ink droplets floating on milk, appeared and bloomed into pupils set in hardened eyes. The jaw lowered to speak, ripping the fused lips apart. A world of suffering horrors was inside its mouth.

"How did a minuscule thing like you come all the way here and infect me with this degradation? Making me a thing of thoughts now. And this cannot change. You came here hoping for murder. Yes, a killing. The heaviest, terrible plan almost fell on me, and I'd be nothing anymore because of you, a speck of life. The suffering is due to all your beings, and eons I have practiced pain to teach, and now I may feel your dread. Come, assassin, your friends will be the first I know."

"Red! Come in, Red! Can you hear us?" Mona shouted into the radio. Everyone watched Red and the star beast on the screen through Puentis' psychic transmission. They held each other, terrified for Red and themselves. "Bring him back!" Mona yelled at Puentis.

"I can't do anything. The star beast is holding him. Red's trapped," Puentis said.

"This is not what we fucking thought was going to happen," Shooda said. "Goddamn it, we created a cosmic super Hitler. Mona, please, what else can we do?"

Mona shook her head. "I don't know. That was everything we had, and the fragment was supposed to kill it, not change it into some humanoid monster. There's no point in sending more fragments or any of you to die. I'm sorry, I let us all down."

"That's not true," Puentis said. "This battle was lost before we began fighting. You have nothing to be sorry about."

The room turned grimly quiet, except for Mona's stifled sobs. Each person was concerned with the impending last moments of their life. Grey nodded to himself, and then his small voice seemed to shatter the air. "Puentis, can you amplify a projected signal through me if I go up there? I would need perhaps a minute, more if you can manage."

"I can do that, but an overlocked projection will tap out all my power," Puentis said. "There's a strong possibility that I won't be able to bring you both back."

"I understand," Grey said, walking to the terminals mounted against the wall. From Grey's wrist, a snake-like cord sprang and connected to a computer socket. "Shooda," Grey called him over. "I'll need your help. Watch me on the live transmission. When I give you the signal, I need you to press this button." Grey pointed at the third eye on his forehead.

Shooda looked confused until he saw the monitor flickering lines of information, and he smiled. "Grey, you crazy motherfucker."

"Red can't hold on much longer. Puentis, I'm ready to go," Grey said, snapping a salute.

Puentis nodded. He lowered into a sitting position to focus his concentration. The terminals began humming powerfully enough to make the walls tremble, warning lights flashing, and Puentis pushed his hands together. "Now go!" Puentis yelled, and Grey's essence soared towards Red.

In space, the star beast twisted Red's body around its fingers like a coin, breaking and reforming Red's muscles and limbs in an agonizing cycle. The sadistic giant wore an empty expression. Red's extreme suffering was hardly an afterthought, and then Grey appeared before him. Grey had transformed into a majestic humanoid figure clad in living armor, as though constructed from an animal of the deepest, darkest abyss.

The star beast actually looked somewhat surprised by Grey's irreverence. Red shouted incoherently at Grey, and the star beast, having remembered him, tossed Red at Grey's feet. "You are an interesting one, an assassin's friend?" the star beast said.

Grey ignored him and turned to Red. "I'm sorry. I would've come faster, but I needed to figure out how to kill him first."

Red tried to speak, but vomited an endless stream of vile creatures.

"Don't worry, it'll be over soon," Grey said.

The star beast snarled. "I know hate for you. It will be unlimited. You are a fool to come here. Your life never dies, always pain, forever my way of killing you." Grey continued disregarding him, and the star beast, filled with a mixture of fascination and rage, lowered himself to see Grey in vivid detail. Grey finally acknowledged the star beast and extended his arm to the side, giving a thumbs-up. The giant was perplexed. Yet, back on Earth, Shooda received the sign and pushed the button on Grey's forehead.

"Puentis, now!" Shooda screamed.

All along Grey's armor, the closed gills and folded fleshy wings sprang open in a fury. Puentis' amplified signal hurtled across the celestial gulf, concentrating into Grey, and the soundwave blasted directly into the star beast's face. The giant recoiled, gripping his head and grinding his teeth. Its flesh undulated in concentric circles under the megaton bass. He smashed the stalagmites around him, and it seemed the entire evil rock was starting to break.

"Such untold power, the frequency of the gods. I cannot defend against this! What weapon do you wield?" the star beast roared.

Grey gently levitated to the star beast's eye level. "It's called funky music."

Grey punched the star beast, and half his head exploded into gore. The massive, ruptured brain grew flailing appendages, attempting to recapture the loosened cerebral chunks that were floating away. Its eyeball came loose and bounced around the head like a squashy medieval flail. The star beast howled and smashed its fists into the ground, erratically twisting its torso so that ribs broke like the trunks of giant sequoias. The star beast broke away from its main body with a final push and shoved off. The half-formed, mutilated torso trailed intestines as it vanished into the dark void.

Grey flew back down to Red. "Damn it, I only wounded him," Grey said.

"Either way, I think you saved us. Look, everything on this rock is dying," Red said. The monstrosities that were fused together lashed out in their death throes. Every demonic face tried to bite the other in futile hopes of cannibalizing some life sustenance. The colossal tentacles curled like old, gnarled trees with dead roots in dry soil. In no time, the drifting horror they stood on transformed into a charnel forest frozen in rigor mortis. Everywhere they looked, stars peacefully shone, and a great silence covered the universe. "Puentis lost our connection. He told me that would likely happen to make this plan work," Grey said. "There is no way to get back."

Red didn't seem bothered. He was too busy looking at a distant planet crossing in front of a nearby star, perhaps the planet's sun. He nodded. "So, funky music. That was a good choice. Only a complete asshole doesn't like funk," Red said. "Don't feel bad. I knew I wouldn't get back even if we succeeded."

Red and Grey were shocked to hear someone clapping behind them and spun around. "You!" Red said.

The star traveler woman smiled at them. "That was really, really incredible. Honestly, I did not expect either of you to live. Just, wow."

"You know this person?" Grey asked.

"Yes, he does. My name is Estrella, the star person," she said. "And I've come to collect my part of a deal. You truly are a wondrous life form, Red, too interesting for there to be only one of you. So, this only works if you agree to be my channel for all the other robots in your homeworld. May we proceed?"

Grey looked at Red. "Hold on, channel? What is she talking about?"

"It happened after I accidentally absorbed Mona's fragment, and you killed me on the rooftop. I met Estrella on the astral plane and made a deal in exchange for the location of Puentis. She wants to make all robots like us, sentient and having free will."

"Every robot? That'll put the world in anarchy," Grey said. "What happens if you refuse to help?"

"I'm not sure I want to refuse," Red said, turning to Estrella. "I'll agree on one condition. Send me and my friend back home."

Estrella flew in a small circle around them and then landed in front of Red, pinching his cheek. "Did you think I'm done with you? Now, please relax and look off at the farthest star you can see. Grey, you, too."

Red experienced a strange sensation in which his body seemed to be phasing into music.

15

he monitors in Puentis' headquarters lost connection shortly after Grey delivered his devastating haymaker. Audio and visual degraded into static. Mona, Shooda, Puentis, and April watched the computers, hoping for any sign that their friends might have survived.

The monitors remained blocks of electric snow long enough to convince them all that Grey and Red's mission was successful, but they weren't coming back.

From space, Estrella allowed this sorrowful spectacle to continue for dramatic purposes. She felt playfully miffed at Red holding their agreement hostage at the last moment and even considered welching on her part after getting what she wanted. That would've taught Red a lesson if he weren't dead. Oh well, she thought, and then smiled. Red and Grey were startled awake in their chairs to the immediate embraces of their friends. Mona even kissed Red, despite him not having any lips.

"That was fun," Estrella said to herself. "Now, to make things so much more interesting."

In the middle of their celebrated reunion, Red noticed that a little screen in the computer terminal had changed channels. A live video showed similar riots occurring in various major cities across different countries. He got up, walked over to the screen, and watched the people and robots clash soundlessly. The laughter died as everyone came over to see what had gotten Red's attention.

At the central plaza, back in New San Diego, the streets were overrun with countless people engaged in some act of violence. Armed mobs hunted down robots among burning cars, the men finally catching them, crushing their heads or laying gunfire into the scurrying robots. Other robots turned their weapons against attackers or committed murder on whoever they could kill. Amid the anarchy, a single robot stumbled through the plaza, looking in bewilderment at the destruction. A lone brick flew through the air and struck the robot on the head, knocking him to the ground. The robot struggled to recompose himself. Through a crack in his face screen, neon fluid dripped and puddled on the ground. Someone yelled, and the robot looked up. A young man, furious and afraid, was pointing a gun at his head. Looking up at the man, the robot dipped his fingers into the radiant fluid and drew a large glowing Enso on his face. The man looked at the robot in utter confusion, hesitating to pull the trigger. They stared at each other for a stunted moment. Finally, the young man opened his mouth to speak just as a large explosion from the building behind him drowned his words.

Shooda pulled Red to face him. "I was right about everything. You always meant for this to happen. We should've never trusted you."

"Shooda, we are alive and have a right to live. Robots can finally think for themselves," Red said. "This isn't war. The violence will settle with enough time."

"You're nothing but a crazy robot."

The room burst into a giant argument. Accusations were hurled at everyone without making any sense. The guards nervously looked to April for the order to pull their weapons. She appeared ready to give it when the screens suddenly turned black and formed one giant red eye. Red immediately recognized Master Robot's voice emitting from every speaker.

"Hello, Red. You have gone much farther than I ever anticipated. You defied my orders, but you've done more for robots than my entire army could have accomplished. This is the second robot revolution. Already, every human nation is thrown into chaos. We'll move forward when the time is ready, and humans will know what it's like to be shackled to their new masters. While you have already served your purpose and have little strategic value, I can use you as a symbol for our new race. Do you understand your mission?"

Everyone watched Red as he walked up to the screen. He stood in front of Master Robot's image and stared directly into the burning eye. "You're talking to a Satin Joker. And we don't take shit from anyone. Puentis, pull his plug. I'm done with this battery-powered fascist."

The screens blinked out dead black.

A few hours later, Red rode out to Louis's solitary ghost town. He dismounted his hover bike and wasn't surprised to find Louis already expecting him at the town's edge. Louis was armed and wearing tactical gear on his upper body, leaving his bare leg exposed to the harsh sun. His boots looked as though he literally tried jumping into them. Louis's beard whipped in the desert wind around his wide smile. He excitedly pointed at Red, "That was you, right? All this is going on everywhere; you made that happen! C'mon, man, tell me it was you."

Red lit a cigarette and took a long drag. He gave Louis a sidelong glance from under his wide-brimmed hat.

"Oh yeah, that's goddamn cool."

Red laughed.

THE END

**STAY TUNED FOR FURTHER
ADVENTURES IN THE
CORE OVERDIE UNIVERSE.**

AUTHOR
ISH GALVAN

Ish Galvan is a Chicano writer and illustrator from North County San Diego. In collaborations with Vince Vargas, he is the co-founder of Triple OG Comics, publisher of "Tamale Guy." He is also the author of "Hidden In The Thorns" and "Blubber Island." Besides making art, he teaches comic book workshops. He's been rumored to have never faked the funk!

SUPER MARIO BROS.
M
EST. IN 1985

ARTIST
MIKE DUBISCH

Over a thirty-year career, Mike Dubisch has illustrated countless books, comics, magazines, and games, specializing in science fiction, horror, and fantasy.

His eerie, timeless artwork has captivated audiences worldwide. The sole illustrator for Forbidden Futures, Dubisch also creates art for tabletop RPGs and collectible card games. Find him on all the socials at @mikedubisch.